Montezuma's Legacy

Professor Blake Fanshaw, accompanied by his feisty daughter, sets out to locate a cave deep within the arid wilderness of south east Utah. It is here that they had hoped to find lost Aztec treasure. Unable to locate the hoard, they become lost amid the maze of canyons. Following a dramatic rescue by reformed outlaw, Lucky Will Brennan, the explorers are destined to meet extraordinary and dangerous characters including the Navaho renegade, Stalking Bear.

Many deaths will haunt the Utah canyon lands before the survivors finally solve the mystery that will forever be referred to as Montezuma's Legacy.

Montezuma's Legacy

Dale Graham

A Black Horse Western

ROBERT HALE · LONDON

© Dale Graham 2004
First published in Great Britain 2004

ISBN 0 7090 7554 5

Robert Hale Limited
Clerkenwell House
Clerkenwell Green
London EC1R 0HT

Typeset by
Derek Doyle & Associates, Liverpool.
Printed and bound in Great Britain by
Antony Rowe Limited, Wiltshire

AUTHOR'S NOTE

Nothing is likely to stir the blood nor quicken the heart-beat more than the lure of hidden treasure. Since time immemorial, secret caches of plunder have enticed bold adventurers to risk their lives in search of the fabled *El Dorado*. Countless dog-eared maps claiming to disclose the whereabouts of untold wealth have been exchanged as frequently as a bad cold. Most have turned out to be the product of a vivid imagination where greed is the prime motivator. Those allegories that have stood the test of time have invariably been absorbed into the national heritage.

One such story handed down by word of mouth testifies to the existence of a fabulous treasure in the White Mountain region of south west Utah near to the town of Kanab. Legend suggests that in the early sixteenth century, the great Aztec ruler Montezuma conveyed vast quantities of gold and jewels there by packhorse from present day Mexico City for safe keeping. The aim was to prevent his nation's wealth falling into the hands of the Spanish conquistadores.

In the beginning, the Aztec people welcomed Hernando Cortés believing him to be a reincarnation of the bearded white-skinned god Quetzalcoatl. A helmet stuffed to the brim with gold dust was offered as a token gesture of welcome to these strange people who sat upon four-legged monsters and carried lightning in their hands. Many more ornate gifts of gold encrusted with precious gems were to follow. Although intended to appease the newcomers, these gifts only served to persuade the fearsome invaders that their wildest dreams had indeed come true.

Only when Montezuma was killed and his 'city of gold' ravaged did the people realize their fatal error of judgement. Abandoning all pretence towards obeisance, the Aztec peoples rose up and set upon their aggressors. Cortés lost most of his army in a single night. Retreating soldiers, overburdened with loot, sank into the surrounding marshland.

But the Spaniards eventually regrouped, proving to be much stronger than the Aztecs. Accordingly, it was only a matter of time before the defeat of this simple race occurred.

Montezuma's successor bowed to the inevitable but not without a final touch of irony. To prevent the national treasure falling into the avaricious hands of his enemies, he was determined to save a substantial portion by having it transported to a far-distant location.

And so began the long trek north through present-day Arizona and into Utah. A journey which culminated in what was thought to be the final resting-place of the legendary *Aztlan*. Few clues were left to suggest where it had been secreted. For the next three centuries, nothing further was heard of this fabulous lost hoard.

Until. . . .

ONE

JOHNSON CANYON

'It has to be around here somewhere.'

The hint of alarm felt by Professor Fanshaw was instantly picked up by his daughter.

'Don't worry, Dad,' she counselled, laying a calming hand on his shoulder. 'If the map indicates a cave entrance in this canyon, then we'll find it.'

Jane Fanshaw was the female equivalent of her father. Tall and statuesque, her russet wavy hair cascaded down over her slim shoulders. At twenty-six, she was the first archaeologist of her sex to have graduated from the University of Chicago. Cynics claimed it was due to the influence of her celebrated father, but both knew she had achieved the honour through sheer grit and determination. A dash of temerity with her superiors had not gone amiss either.

Potential suitors, of which there was no dearth, vied for the chance of walking out with the beautiful young achiever. All had fallen by the wayside. Unable to meet her exacting standards with regard to both intellect and the social graces, they had given up in favour of more gullible

7

conquests. A feisty girl keen to promote the rights of women, she had boldly encouraged Blake Fanshaw with his latest expedition to uncover a lost hoard of Aztec gold.

'Let me have a look,' suggested Jane following Blake along the base of the towering wall of red sandstone that hemmed them into the gloomy rift. She took the proffered map. It was a copy taken from what was intimated to be the original dating back more than three centuries. Peering closely at the spidery depiction, her large round eyes narrowed to thin slits, perfectly matching the cobalt sky. 'Pass me the compass!'

Her father, well used to the brusque nature of his daughter 'in the field', gave a loose smile before complying.

Her eyes flicked between map and compass. Eventually, a long elegant digit prodded the map.

'We're in the wrong canyon,' she announced firmly. 'This one heads due north. The one we want breaks west up ahead.' She pointed a delicate finger along the narrow twisting trail they were following. Her keen-eyed gaze attempted to pierce the hazy ochre of the narrow split. Then, with a careless shrug, she shifted the weight of her backpack and set off along the stony floor. 'Another hundred yards and we should know one way or the other,' she said, leading the way.

Blake was happy to hand the reins over to his daughter. Just like her mother, he thought. Rachel would have been proud of the girl, had she survived the merciless typhoid epidemic that had swept through Chicago back in '66. Jane was only ten when the tragedy struck. And it had been left to Blake to raise his daughter amidst the organized chaos of numerous archaeology digs. It was automatically assumed that the sprightly youngster would eventually follow him into the profession.

A tear hovered on the edge of his eyelid. He wiped it away with the sleeve of his beige tunic, thankful that he was behind the girl. It wouldn't do for a father to be seen blubbing out here in the wilderness of south-west Utah.

Blake looked around. It was indeed a bleak spot. Sagebrush and desiccated thorn vied for the meagre light filtering down between the hard unyielding bluffs that almost met overhead. It was a miracle that primitive Indians had found their way here all those years previously with what was reputed to be a vast pack-train laden with untold wealth.

Like so many of Blake Fanshaw's archaeological discoveries, luck had played a major part in his current expedition. An avid pursuer of all things Aztec from an early age, he had been searching for documentation in Mexico City's famous Museum of Antiquities during the previous spring of 1882.

Only by chance during a break from his work had he come across an ancient manuscript in a junk-shop hidden away down a smelly back street off the central plaza. And secreted within the leather covering that had worked loose was a map indicating the location of Montezuma's legendary cache. Until then it had been shrugged off as a mere chimera, just another mystery created by past generations to add spice to the Aztec heritage. But this find had the stamp of authenticity, the genuine article.

There was only one way to find out.

So here they were. Fifteen miles east of Kanab, the nearest town of any size. This was the first time that either of them had visited the newly opened western frontier of the United States. Offers from locals to guide the pair of greenhorns into the 'canyonlands' were met with snooty disdain by both parties.

If Blake Fanshaw could lead successful expeditions up the Ohio River, through the Cumberland Gap and over the Appalachian Divide, then this brief recce would be child's play. Sneers and guffaws behind their backs only served to strengthen their resolve. In any case, Blake was astute enough to realize that any mention of hidden gold was bound to attract unwanted attention from ruffians and bandits known to frequent these frontier townships.

This morning the pair had set off alone on mounts hired from the livery stable. Virtually the whole town of 527 souls had turned out to witness and deride the departure of the two intrepid explorers.

'Don't git lost!' shouted a voice from the crowd.

'Watch out fer any stray rattlers,' from another. Raucous laughter pursued them down the main street.

Riding stiffly with heads held high, both father and daughter paid little heed as they nudged their horses eastwards along the rough trail *en route* to their objective. Locating the Crawdaddy Breaks had been easy enough. The hotel owner had offered directions to his guests and told them of a distinctive rock boasting the profile of a human face. Known as Indian Butte, it guarded the confined entrance to the maze of canyons. Johnson Canyon was but one of innumerable cragfast ravines. Here they had been forced to tether the horses.

A trek of two hours had followed. The narrow constricted trail climbed steeply before dropping down into the heart of the red massif. Advancing slowly on foot, they soon began to understand why so many people had been derisive of their intention to go it alone. The day was hot. But the enclosed nature of the terrain only served to amplify the effects of the blistering heat.

With a sigh of relief, Jane recognized the subsidiary crack in the weathered rock plateau. Spiny tendrils of

10

mesquite plucked at exposed flesh delivering an array of scratches as the intrepid duo pushed through the thick barrier of vegetation. A quick glance was enough to show that nobody had obviously passed this way for some considerable time.

That discovery alone was sufficient to generate a second wind.

'Not far now,' called out Jane on hearing her father's wheezing breath.

This sort of terrain was far more difficult than even Blake could ever have imagined. No wonder it had taken so long to settle these western territories. He paused for a second to loosen his shirt-collar. The single-lens monocle glinted in the afternoon sun.

He looked up at the overhanging ramparts. And that was when he saw it.

Being three inches taller than his daughter had enabled the ageing professor to see the lethal predator wriggling angrily on a rock ledge immediately to her left. Its ugly flat head was raised, twisting and swaying amid the swirl of deadly coils no more than twelve inches away from and level with her sleek features. The vibrations made by their tired approach must have disturbed it. And it was a big one.

'Stop!' he shouted from just behind. 'Don't move a muscle.'

Instantly the girl halted, receptive to the animated panic in her father's guttural tone. That was when Jane Fanshaw became aware of the steady clicking of the rattlesnake's tail bones. It was the first time she had heard the deadly chatter. An icy tingle slid down her spine, blood pounding in her head. And that was when she knew the taste of pure fear.

'Keep absolutely still whilst I distract him,' continued

Blake in a choking rasp. 'Soon as I give the word, dive to your right.'

The girl uttered a hoarse croak, an all too fearful indication that she understood. A faint breeze disturbed the loose sand on the ledge, further irritating the deadly predator. Its rattle increased as the lethal poison-packers revealed themselves, venom dripping ominously from the razored points.

Hardly daring to breathe lest he antagonize the creature, Blake carefully removed his safari bush hat, a battered relic from many previous expeditions. Measuring the distance at no more than six feet, he tried desperately to replay in his mind the prowess he had achieved on fairground hoop-la stalls of his youth back in Virginia. A sliding, sideways motion using wrist action. He would only have one chance, and he had to get it just right, or else . . .

The alternative didn't bear contemplating. It was now or never. A sharp intake of breath, hold it, then flick.

'Now!' he yelled as the hat spun across the intervening space to cover the lunging head. The snake's elongated body wound itself round the beige felt, the deadly fangs buried deep in the material.

Scrambling away from the bizarre contortions displayed by the crazed reptile, Jane staggered to her feet assisted by her anxious father. Eyes bulged, unable to drag themselves from the gruesome scenario. Her breath exhaled in pained gasps on realizing how close she had come to a fatal injection from one of the most feared of desert creatures.

Once the snake realized there was no danger or meal to be had from the old hat, it emitted a final hiss of contempt and slithered away into the shelter of the rocks.

'That was a close shave and no mistake,' uttered Blake making no move to retrieve his beloved *chapeau*. After this escapade, he had no wish to wear it ever again. The thick iron-grey hair would have to be sufficient protection from the gruelling heat of the sun. He dragged an arm carelessly across a sweaty forehead.

'We need a short rest if only to calm our jangled nerves.' He sighed slumping against a rock.

Blake removed his pack and offered his daughter the water bottle. Already it was half-empty. And they hadn't seen a trace of the life-giving fluid since entering the warren of canyons some three hours earlier. His daughter slurped greedily, but Blake hadn't the heart to restrain her need.

It was a full half-hour before they felt able to continue. Jane nervously scanned every rock and shadowy recess for further danger as they slowly moved further into the branch canyon.

Blake searched the base of the towering rock-face to their left.

Suddenly he stopped and pointed to a darkened recess in the impenetrable wall fifty feet above the canyon floor.

'That's it!' he exclaimed, his mahogany tones cracking with suppressed excitement. 'Up there. Beyond that patch of juniper. The entrance to a cave.'

Leaving the main trail, the pair of explorers scrambled feverishly over the sea of loose rock scree that littered the base of the cliff. On reaching the vertical rock face, a clear entrance eight feet high and five wide revealed itself.

Father and daughter held each other's gaze, knowing they were on the brink of a momentous discovery.

Blake removed a tallow brand from his pack and lit up. Leading the way, he moved gingerly along the constricted passage. Moisture dripped from the roof in marked contrast to the arid nature of the sun-baked exterior. After five minutes, the torch revealed a series of cave paintings below which was a tract of writing in the ancient picture language favoured by the Aztec peoples.

That was sufficient proof that this was the right cave.

'Can you read it?' enquired Jane excitedly, pressing forward. The recent near fatal incident was forgotten as the culmination of their endeavours seemed close.

Blake held the torch steady. 'The drawings indicate a vast movement.' His finger sketched a path along the faded outline. 'Mules carrying heavy loads.' He paused, drawing out the meaning of the strange depictions. Then he slowly translated. '*Those who follow after bearing false image will discover their true worth. And Montezuma will have his revenge.*'

'What does it mean?'

Jane's obvious puzzlement elicited a shrug from her father. Slowly and precisely he repeated the strange enigmatic depiction.

'Perhaps it refers to the Spanish deception, the notion that the European invaders represented gods to be deified. And the revenge, of course, points to the removal of the treasure so it would not fall into their avaricious hands.' His gnarled brow creased in puzzlement, not least because the passage here came to an abrupt termination.

Not a natural ending of solid rock, it had been deliberately blocked off to deter interlopers such as themselves. There was no way they could make further progress without the assistance of extra labour. It was a disappointment, but one Blake knew he should have anticipated.

The flickering yellow from the torch reflected the frustration in his green eyes. His full lips puckered with annoyance, the wide mouth drooping at one side.

'What next?' from Jane.

Ignoring the question, he turned retracing his steps to the entrance, followed closely by his daughter. Outside a baking globe of orange beamed down, spearing them with its ferocity. It was a cogent reminder of how energy-sapping archaeological digs in remote theatres could be.

Jane tugged at her father's tailored buckskin jacket, repeating her query as to what their next move should be. Blake pulled out his clay mearschaum and lit up before answering. A few good draws on the curved pipe always helped to concentrate his thoughts.

'It is now imperative that we first return to Kanab,' he stated slowly, 'then take the earliest train west to liaise with Benjamin.'

Ben Cassidy was Jane's fiancé. He had agreed to meet them at the town of Beaver Creek, a day's train-ride west of Kanab. The small rail station had developed into some-thing of a boom town since the opening of the Grand Union branch line south from Reno.

Specifically built to encourage new settlement of the barren wasteland, the gamble financed by the Cassidy Meat Packing Corporation of Chicago had proved to be a resounding success. Ben was the president's only son and had taken over much of the day-to-day running of the company from his ageing father.

'We can then arrange to hire the appropriate men and equipment to break through the cave barrier,' continued Blake. 'That's the only way we can fully explore the inner sanctum.'

'And hopefully secure the lost treasure of Montezuma,' added Jane in a rather sceptical tone. All this scrabbling about in the remote wilderness of Utah was beginning to pall. Muttering under her breath, she appended the fervent aspiration that it would end very soon, so that they could all return to the civilized trappings of Chicago.

Scrambling back over the loose mantle of scree down into the ravine, they headed back towards the main canyon. After a half-hour it was Jane who voiced the fears that both were feeling.

'We ought to have struck the main trail through Johnson Canyon by now. I don't recognize this one at all.'

'That's because all this terrain looks the same,' replied Blake, removing his necker and wiping the sweat from his forehead. 'I figure if we backtrack a-ways, we're bound to meet up with the main trail where the horses are tethered.' The confident assertion was made with a sombre feeling that he made sure to keep well hidden.

Another hour passed before Blake was forced to admit the inevitable.

'We're lost, aren't we?' enquired his daughter, her normally serene countenance creased with worry. Equally tired and dispirited, unable to maintain an optimistic guise any longer, her father merely nodded.

Jane sat down on a rock and uncorked the water bottle. A couple of drops sizzling on her leathery tongue only served to exacerbate a raging thirst. Blake offered his own bottle which still held a few warm mouthfuls. Jane looked at him silently, then at the bottle. Her body felt as if it was being slowly broiled in the unremitting heat. Sorely tempted she reached out, then checked herself.

No!

Their only hope now lay in finding a hidden spring, if such an oasis existed in this brutally arid landscape. She stood up, swaying with fatigue. At that moment she would have gladly surrendered all the gold in the world for a jug full of cold water. Eyes tightly clenched to blot out the blinding glare reflected off the canyon walls, Jane's water-starved brain whirled like a spinning top.

Blake grabbed at his daughter's coat to prevent her falling.

'Careful, my dear. We'll find a way out of this labyrinth.'
That was when he heard it.

A throaty growl, low yet menacing, assailed his hearing.
Even in her blurred state, Jane had also heard the threatening snarl. Out of the corner of his left eye, Blake sensed a movement. He turned to face this new danger, firmly pushing his daughter behind him. A strangled gasp escaped from his parched lips.

Black and piercing, a pair of huge staring eyes skewered him to the spot. Pawing the ground a mountain lion, sleek yet deadly, was preparing to launch itself at this pair of biped interlopers. Again it emitted a rancorous snarl. A vicious set of gleaming snappers smiled as this ultimate predator flexed its haunches edging closer in readiness for the kill.

Backing off, eyes fastened on to the advancing creature, father and daughter stood little chance against such an efficient killing machine. With no weapon to hand, they were at its mercy. Of which, they could be certain, precious little would be forthcoming.

TWO

CHANCE
ENCOUNTERS

Nudging thirty, Will Brennan, tall and rangy with a mane of thick dark hair, reined in the paint and levered himself out of the saddle.

'Time to call it a day,' he said, addressing his comment to the sleek equine. 'What d'you reckon, Chase? Water for you, and a brew of the finest Java for me.' The horse snickered in agreement. 'Then we'll see about cookin' up some grub.'

Will stepped down and stretched, easing the cramp from weary muscles. On the move since sun-up without a break, both man and cayuse were sore in need of rest and revitalization.

His intended destination was Carson City in Nevada, where rumours abounded concerning a new gold strike. Perhaps for once, lady luck would see fit to pay him more than a passing glance. And Will felt he was badly in need of a change in fortune following a recent unhappy interlude on the wrong side of the law.

That was his reason for choosing to ride these back trails across the state of Utah. Few people intentionally opted to ride the canyonlands where stories of travellers coming to a sticky end had become legendary. Only Indians and lawbenders on the dodge took their chances amidst the sweltering maze of arid gorges that comprised the Crawdaddy Breaks.

And Will Brennan had no wish to encounter any dude sporting a tin star on his vest. He scanned the surrounding brush for hidden critters that might take umbrage to his presence, then set about making camp for the night. After gathering twigs to establish a fire for his supper of fatback and beans, Will sat down, leaned against his saddle and rolled a quirly. He slid his tongue along the gummed paper's edge, scratched a vesta over his Levis and applied the flame.

It never reached the thin tobacco cylinder.

A terrified scream broke into his dreamy ruminations. Echoing down the enclosed confines of the arroyo, it brought Will instantly to his feet and reaching for the revolver at his hip. The shriek was followed immediately by a brutal snarl that he recognized as that emanating from an angry cougar.

A lowering frown, tense and alert, scored his dark features. The forgotten quirly dropped from pursed lips as he whipped out the Colt Frontier and thumbed back the hammer. That was no squeal of fright from some wild creature.

It was human – and female.

Centring on the direction from which the blood-curdling halloo had originated, Will clambered to his feet and hot-footed down to the end of the dry wash, dodging the lunging tentacles of spiny thornbush. Another

19

rancorous growl split the ether. This time it was closer and to his left on the far side of a low knoll. Boot soles slipped as he clawed a path up the loose shale. He grabbed a branch sticking out from a crack in the rock and hauled himself over the crest.

There below, at the end of a box ravine, a girl and an older man cowered against the back wall. The man, a strange dude having the aura of a latter-day Robert E Lee and clad in a beige suit, picked up a stone and threw it at the advancing threat. It clipped the animal's hind leg, serving merely to further enrage the creature.

Will could see it was about to leap across the intervening space. A distance of no more than ten feet.

He hesitated for a split second as the animal launched itself.

In mid-flight, cruel white claws stretching to gouge and maim, the elongated body jerked violently as a pair of harsh cracks rent the air. Blood spurted from two punctures in the lumbar region. The lion twitched and wriggled as it crashed to earth at the feet of the trapped duo.

Although badly wounded, the creature still had some fight left. A last growl of rage and it staggered up and lunged at the girl. Another two shots rang out, but not before a jagged claw ripped through the girl's trouser and down her leg as gnashing incisors desperately tried to do their worst.

After scrambling down from his rocky perch, Will almost reluctantly emptied his revolver into the twitching beast from point blank-range. Only then did it finally surrender and lie still.

'He put up a darned good fight,' muttered Will half to himself as he thumbed fresh cartridges into the chambers of his pistol. 'It took a full load to finish him.' The grudging respect shown to the beast that had nearly killed her educed a choked response from Jane Fanshaw.

'How can you say that when that . . . that *thing* almost killed us,' she snapped, aiming the caustic retort at their saviour whilst attempting to stanch the flow of blood from her gouged leg.

'This is his territory, ma'am,' said Will. 'He's only protectin' his patch. It's you what's the trespasser.'

'Ugh!' exclaimed the girl churlishly.

Her father quickly stepped in to calm the potential outburst.

'We want to thank you, stranger, for coming to our rescue.' Blake gave his daughter a cautionary look before continuing. 'Please excuse my daughter's petulant manner. All this has been hard on us both.'

Will nodded his understanding.

'If it hadn't been for you happening along when you did, we'd have ended our days on this creature's dinner plate. And not only that, we've lost our way.' The archaeologist ran a hand through the tangle of silvery hair as he peered ruefully up at the looming walls of the canyon. Then he turned back to Will. 'My name is Blake Fanshaw,' he said, 'and this is my daughter Jane.'

'Will Brennan,' replied their saviour, accepting the proffered hand. 'Some people call me Lucky.'

'Today I think it's us that are the lucky ones,' answered Blake Fanshaw, smiling. 'I never figured this country could be so huge and threatening.'

Will had meanwhile bent down to examine the sassy female's injury.

'You'll live,' he said casually, tying his bandanna around the three-inch gash. 'It's only a flesh wound. Looks a lot worse than it is.' Then he helped the girl to her feet. 'Hold on to my arm until we reach my camp. It's not far.'

His attempt to help the girl met with a curt rebuttal.

'I can manage, thank you.'

Will shrugged, catching her father's raised eyebrow which silently evinced an apology for his feisty kin. But as soon as he left Jane to her own devices, she stumbled to the ground with a pained cry.

That was when the release of pent-up tears ensued. This time, she accepted the thoughtful stranger's assistance. The languid appeal in her large green eyes were all the thanks he needed.

Once they had reached Will's camp, he left them and backtracked to locate the unlikely pair's missing horses. By the time he had returned, the light was fading allowing dark shadows to creep along the arroyo bottom. A fiery backdrop slowly paled to a deep purple as the sun dropped below the serrated ridge.

Following a simple meal, Will ensured that the fire was well built up to discourage any other night prowlers from making their presence felt. Facing the others across the flickering wisps of orange flame, he posed the question as to why such obvious strangers to the Western frontier were wandering alone in this unforgiving wilderness.

'This sure ain't the kinda country to git yourselves lost in,' he stressed, sipping at his mug of coffee. He pulled hard on the now recovered quirley, discharging a plume of blue smoke into the darkness. 'You must have good reason fer bein' here.'

Will noticed the quick glance that flashed between father and daughter. Like himself, it appeared they had something to hide.

Blake coughed to give himself time to think. The fire-light reflected off his monocle.

'We are archaeologists from Chicago,' he began, declining a roll-up from his host in favour of the strange clay pipe. 'We've come out West to investigate the presence of an ancient cave in this part of the state. It is reputed to contain an array of artefacts dating from the period of Aztec civilization in Mexico.'

He went on to explain the legend of Montezuma in full, purposely omitting any mention of the vast hoard of gold they hoped to uncover. No sense in drawing unnecessary attention to their true purpose. After all, they might be grateful to this handsome stranger for saving their lives, but what did they know about him?

Nothing.

And if they had known the course that Will Brennan's life had taken over the last few years, they would have been more than a little perturbed at the type of man with whom they were sharing a meal.

After he had finished, Professor Fanshaw peered over the glowing embers waiting for the other to respond. A heavy silence followed.

'It was most opportune for us that you came along when you did, Mr Brennan,' purred Jane in a voice like melted chocolate. 'But what brings you to this uncivilized part of the country?' Curling her graceful eyebrows, Jane Fanshaw smiled with unknowing suggestiveness.

Any other time and Will Brennan would have been stirred by the deep pools of light that held his gaze. But his thoughts had drifted off into the night, back to another time. Gazing into the flickering embers, malevolent spirits from a tormented past bestirred his soul, haunting the very essence of his being.

It had all begun five years before. Back in 1877, Will Brennan was a contented if rather poor man. Riding shotgun for Wells Fargo was dangerous work and the rewards were scant. But that didn't bother the young man. He enjoyed the adventurous life guarding the company's payroll shipments on stage runs between Tucson, in Arizona territory, north to Salt Lake City, Utah.

On a couple of occasions the line had been hit by road agents. But so far, due primarily to the shooting prowess of the young guard, there had been no losses and the badhats had been effectively driven off with their tails between their legs.

Then rumours began circulating along the route that Will Brennan was being earmarked for greater things, promotion to line manager with his own office. Yes indeed, life appeared to be moving in the right direction, especially now that he'd met the girl he hoped to marry.

Ellie Summers was the banker's daughter in Tucson and Orville Summers had been more than willing to confirm the union when the up-and-coming Wells Fargo man had sought his consent.

That was the day before his twenty-fifth birthday. Encouraged by friends and colleagues to celebrate such good fortune in both his professional and personal circumstances, Will was frog-marched round all the saloons in town. Unused to strong liquor, Will was later to claim ignorance as to how he eventually awoke the next morning beside a lady of the night in Lulubelle's, the most notorious of Tucson's seedy whorehouses.

Unfortunately, his employers, strict temperance adherents, refused to accept Will's excuses. Being incapable of taking out the morning run was bad enough. When drink and loose morals were found to be the cause, the company's rules were adamant. Such behaviour was felt to be incompatible with the career of a budding manager

24

with the Wells Fargo Stagecoach Company. His services were instantly dispensed with.

Word of the disgrace spread like wildfire. Suddenly finding himself without a job, Will was ostracized from the upper echelons of Tucson society. Worst of all, he was unceremoniously dropped by the girl he thought would stand by him no matter what the circumstances. She had refused even to see him, no doubt at the insistence of her father.

There was no other option then but for him to leave town.

A visit to the bank for the purpose of withdrawing what meagre savings he had accrued was to prove Will Brennan's undoing.

His mind was spinning as he entered the front door, struggling to figure out where he would head for. Maybe another stage line would take him on. But without a suitable reference, the odds were stacked against that possibility.

Closing the door, he sensed that something in the bank was different, not as it should be.

Then it struck him. The blinds were still drawn down over the windows. In the middle of the day? That couldn't be right. Only when he saw the guns held by what he had thought were customers did it register that he had walked in on a hold-up.

Eyes bulging, his gaze quickly absorbed the bizarre interchange between a big man dressed in black from head to toe and the bank teller. The robbers hadn't seen him yet, their attention completely taken with persuading the terrified man to open up the safe.

'But I can't open the safe,' pleaded the quaking teller. 'It's on a time lock.'

'Don't give me that eyewash,' snarled the man in black,

brandishing a deadly sawn-off shotgun. 'Just get it open, pronto, and hand over the cash if'n you don't want a gutful of lead.'

Quietly, Will drew his revolver. That was his second mistake. At that precise moment, a guard employed by the bank emerged from a side door.

'What in tarnation's goin' on here,' he shouted, levelling his pistol. Face to face with Will, the guard mistook him for one of the robbers.

Flame spat twice, the first bullet punching Will back against the door whilst the second took one of the gang in the head, killing him instantly.

As the raiders spun to face this unexpected threat, the bank teller ducked into the back office containing the safe and locked the door. Before the guard was able to fire again, the man in black spun round shooting him in the stomach. Doubling over, the injured guard slumped to the floor moaning in agony.

'You reckoned this would be an easy bank to crack,' complained a surly youth backing towards the outer door, his sixgun swinging wildly.

'That's the way it should have been,' snapped the big man, 'but this ain't no time to argue the toss.'

Realizing their chance had gone, the robbers panicked and fled, taking Will Brennan with them. At the time his throbbing shoulder made any reasoning as to the cause of this bizarre situation impossible. He just allowed himself to be led away on the dead robber's mount.

Dusky shadows of evening had crept into the arid badlands of the Sierrita Mountains south-west of Tucson before the gang were safely back in their hideout. Only then did Will discover that, far from resenting his intrusion into their failed attempt to rob the Tucson bank, the bandits were grateful for his timely intervention.

Unwittingly he had prevented a savage gun battle and the gang's certain capture, or even death. Quick on the uptake, he readily concurred with their assumption that he himself was a road agent who had inadvertently butted in on a rival gang's domain.

It was some weeks before Will's shoulder had fully healed.

Mace Cavanagh, oldest of the bunch and a grizzled veteran of the Civil War was an expert fixer when it came to gunshot wounds. Attached to the Sixth Ohio Volunteers as a medic, he had proved his worth to the gang on numerous occasions. And Will was beholden to the ageing desperado for the care he had exercised when removing the slug. A few shots of redeye and the new recruit had barely felt the heated blade digging into his injured shoulder.

During that time the gang had only pulled one other job. But their attempt to rob the Nogales stage had netted only loose change from the passengers.

Duke Miller was fuming.

'Seems like every time we plan a job, somethin' goes wrong,' he complained, slamming a fist on the deal table inside the two-roomed shack. 'What I need is some real inside information.'

'What d'yuh mean, boss?' asked a young bad-ass everyone called the Brazos Kid. His real name was Hyram. Though anybody stupid enough to call him that was likely to receive a deadly dose of lead poisoning for their folly.

As the smallest kid in his class, the Kid had been forced to endure hurtful comments and bullying from so-called friends back in his home town of Marlin, east Texas. The taunts had ended abruptly on his sixteenth birthday when the Kid acquired his first six-shooter. A present from his father, the ancient cap-and-ball Remington had answered back with fatal consequences.

There was no other option but to leave Marlin in double-quick time. And from that day, Hyram Goodloving had become known as the Brazos Kid.

Duke Miller grabbed a bottle of whiskey, sunk a hefty slug, then roughly wiped the drips from his black moustache before answering.

'I know for sure that the mining companies transport their payroll by stagecoach. Yet every time we try to lift it, they ain't totin' no damn blasted strongbox.'

He scowled darkly removing a rolled stogie from his black leather vest. It matched the rest of his attire, now somewhat dust-stained following the hard ride back into the safety of the Sierritas. 'It appears as if they know where and when the friggin' hold-up's gonna take place.'

'Maybe we oughta think about headin' east into New Mexico,' suggested a stocky bald-headed jasper. 'I hear tell there's been a silver strike along the Mimbres.'

Wild Cat Wilson scratched at his grubby one-piece undershirt. In build he was akin to a brick privy and just as smelly, but it was the purple scar staining the whole left side of his ugly visage that first announced itself to newcomers.

Anybody foolish enough to ogle the birthmark was more than likely to earn themselves a feline snarl pursued by the wild man's hamlike fists. He fingered the itchy scar that always seemed to make its presence felt in the early hours of the day.

'If we were to keep our eyes 'n ears peeled, we could muscle in on some easy paydirt,' he added with a mirthless grimace.

Miller grunted, tugging on his moustache, deep in thought.

'Maybe,' he muttered, hawking a gob of phlegm into the stone grate. 'Sure as hell we gotta do somethin'.'

Will Brennan had been listening to the exchange with interest. Through no fault of his own, he had found himself thrown into the bearpit with this bunch of desperadoes. Not a situation he would have chosen as a career option, he was nonetheless quite willing to see how things panned out.

And only the day before, his newly acquired profession had been given an added boost. Returning from a trip down to the small town of San Xavier for supplies, Mace Cavanagh had brought back a wanted poster with their new recruit's detailed description and mugshot.

'Take a look at this, boys,' he had crowed, busting through the shack door and throwing the sheet on to the table for all to see. 'Brennan here has gotten hisself a reputation.' He jabbed excitedly at the sum posted for Will's apprehension. 'A thousand bucks! That's more'n Wild Cat 'n the Kid together.'

'Let me see that,' growled the sceptical young rannigan, grabbing the poster. He snorted in disgust. 'How come this dude is so popular with the law. He ain't done nothin' yet. Some jiggers have all the luck.'

Cavanagh chuckled gleefully. 'That's right, Brazos. Don't they just.' Then slapping Will playfully on the back he hollered: 'Luck sure is the word for you, mister. Lucky Brennan! That's what you are.'

And from there on Will Brennan became *Lucky* Brennan.

So here he was, stuck in a grubby shack on the run from the law with a price on his head he didn't deserve, nor one that he had sought. Seeing as how he had been saddled with an owlhooter's label, Will figured he might as well play the part. At the same time, it would provide the opportunity to avenge himself on the company that had made him a fugitive from the law.

Yes indeed, Wells Fargo would pay dearly for treating this particular loyal employee in the manner of some low-life pariah.

Having made his decision, Lucky Brennan offered more than just his gun hand to the outlaw gang. Duke Miller had not made any enquiries into Brennan's past. He naturally assumed their latest recruit was in the same line of work, so to speak. And his unlikely appearance had come at just the right moment. He could replace Esteban Mendoza – the gunnie shot and killed during the bank hold-up at Tucson.

'No need for quittin' the state,' offered Lucky in a low, even tone that found the other members of the gang eyeing him keenly.

'You know somethin' we don't?' snapped Miller aggressively, his knuckles blanching as he gripped the table. He was in no mood for idle comments.

The new recruit held his gaze whilst lighting up a cheroot. Smoke lifted from the brown tube before he replied.

'It's not that Wells Fargo know what your next move is gonna be, Duke. But shipments are transferred to the banks on irregular runs so as to foil any potential robberies.'

'If that's the case, how can you help,' responded Miller with a waspish inflection.

'Any transit of gold has to be well organized if it's to succeed,' replied Lucky. smiling, 'and someone has to do that organizin' – create a plan of action if yuh see what I mean.'

Duke Miller frowned. Frustration at being constantly duped had clouded his normally astute brain. With an unexpected sweep, the table crashed back as he leapt to his feet, a lethal shooter suddenly appearing in a black-gloved right hand.

'Don't play games with me, mister,' he rasped hoarsely, jabbing the deadly snout of the weapon at Lucky Brennan's head. 'Spit out what yuh gotta say, pronto.'

The burst of temper saw the other members of the gang stiffening, hands poised over their guns. Only Brennan remained calm, unruffled. He knew that the destiny of this bunch of wastrels was effectively in his hands. He also knew that revealing his past association with Wells Fargo might brand him a spy.

Still holding Miller's fixed glare, his face broke into a languid smile, another plume of blue smoke sidling from the corner of his mouth.

That was when Miller finally caught on.

'You!' he exclaimed. 'You planned the transit rosters.'

Lucky gave an easy nod.

'So you're party to every shipment in and out of Tucson?'

'That's what it amounts to.'

'So how come you ended up on the owlhooter's trail?' rasped Brazos, close to Will's ear. Will recounted how his career with the company had come to an untimely end. The disclosure encouraged the others to believe that was the reason he was now on the wrong side of the law. Following his revelation, Will held his breath. His continued intake of oxygen now depended on Miller's reaction to the outlandish story.

Time hung heavy in the smoky cabin. One minute seemed like an hour. Then the gang leader pronounced judgement.

31

'Darned if I ain't the luckiest son-of-a-sidewinder to have been landed with you.' Miller's taut features relaxed, along with those of the rest of the gang. With a broad grin, he offered the bottle of hooch to Brennan.

'Missed yer chance there, boss,' piped up Cavanagh, 'It'd be mighty confusin' if we had two *Luckys* in the gang.'

The tense atmosphere instantly eased, Miller leading a chorus of raucous laughter.

THREE

UNLUCKY BRENNAN

That was the start of a successful run of stage hold-ups over the next few months. The gang became known as the *Arizona Blackhawks*, after their leader's dark attire, and they revelled in the notoriety such acclaim brought. Each member of the gang found the price on his head increasing dramatically. Not surprisingly, it was Lucky Brennan who became the most valuable.

But all good things invariably come to an end.

Wells Fargo eventually came to the conclusion that somebody had to be supplying the bandits with information about shipments. Everybody in the company came under suspicion. It never occurred to the directors that their ex-employee, Will Brennan, was the cause of all their problems. So it was inevitable that major changes were forthcoming.

Rosters were altered, new routes devised, and extra guards posted.

The easy pickings promised and previously delivered by

Brennan now began to dry up. Robbing female passengers of their miserly poke held no glamour for Duke Miller. Jittery and apprehensive, jumping at every shadow, a taut edginess had crept into his demeanour. The gang became restless, ill-tempered.

And with that came a degree of desperation that was sure to end in terminal gunplay. The Brazos Kid had begun to exercise his trigger finger more than previously. Always a hothead, he had thus far refrained from putting anybody in boot hill.

Even the imperturbable Mace Cavanagh began cleaning his hardware more than was the norm, constantly searching the horizon beyond the confines of the hideout. Cavanagh was sure that any day now pursuing law-enforcement agents employed by Wells Fargo would locate their hideout.

Duke Miller and Cavanagh had been together a long while. The gang boss had faith in the ageing gunfighter's intuition. He sensed that the gang's days hidden away within the security of the wild Sierrita fastness were numbered. Days of riding out like a latter-day Dick Turpin to rob passing stagecoaches, then disappearing into the sandy wasteland, were rapidly drawing to a close.

They had looked to Lucky Will Brennan for the solution. But luck appeared to have run out for the ex-bullion guard. He had no way of ascertaining the vital information required. And with the gang's ill-gotten gains rapidly dwindling, Lucky sensed a matching loss of confidence in his abilities.

As with most outlaw gangs, loot was soon frittered away on other more important callings such as girls, booze and gambling. A constant supply was needed just to maintain the status quo.

One day whilst Brennan was out hunting for their next meal, Brazos voiced the concerns the others were also thinking.

'Ain't no use havin' that guy on the payroll if he can't deliver the goods,' he complained aiming his remark at Duke Miller.

The gang leader frowned, his black bushy eyebrows meeting in the middle of his forehead giving him the appearance of a predatory eagle.

To emphasize his disquiet, the Kid threw his tin plate of refried beans into the fire. The orange mess hissed and sizzled in the ashes.

'And I'm sick of havin' to shovel down that slop,' he added belligerently, challenging anyone to disagree. It didn't help that it was over a week since any of the gang had eaten any meat.

A grunt of agreement came from Cavanagh sprawled on his bunk in the corner.

'Sure as eggs is eggs, we need us a fresh angle,' he said crinkling his eyes in thought. 'Maybe we oughta quit Arizona and head north, rob us a train eh?' He sat up scratching his thinning grey thatch. 'I hear tell the James boys done well over in Missouri. It wouldn't need more'n the four of us.'

Miller nodded slowly. 'Could be you got a point there, Mace,' he murmured. 'Which is the nearest railroad from here?'

'The Grand Union branch line, six, maybe seven days' ride to the north,' replied Cavanagh eagerly.

'We ain't never done a train afore,' challenged Wilson, clawing at his peeling scalp.

'Scared are yuh?' The sneering remark from the Kid saw Wild Cat Wilson lunging for the young rannie, a hefty right poised to wipe the smirk from the Kid's spotty face.

Only the quick intervention of Miller prevented blood and more being spilled.

'Cut the gripin',' he growled, prodding each of his well-oiled Colt .45 Peacemakers under the chins of the two aggressors. 'I'll decide what jobs we pull, savvy?'

An encouraging jab from the gleaming revolvers secured an uneasy truce.

'We'll give tomorrow's stage one more shot,' declared Miller stiffly. 'Then if that don't pay off . . .'

Further mutterings and whispered comments were quickly stifled when Will appeared in the doorway, in his hand a dead rattler.

'Afraid it was all I could find,' he apologized.

The recent flare-up was forgotten as Brazos emitted a disgusted snort and pushed past the hunter out of the cabin. Stewed diamondback and refried beans didn't bear thinking about.

A heavy silence followed. Will tried to dismiss the brooding atmosphere with a nonchalant shrug but he clearly sensed that his days as a member of the Arizona Blackhawks might well be numbered.

The following day at noon the gang assembled where the trail narrowed at Klondyke Gulch, an ideal spot for a hold-up. As the stagecoach was forced to slow up at the tight bend, the masked raiders jumped out, brandishing their hardware. Strangely, they found the driver to be more than a little co-operative, compliant even.

All went well until the strongbox was forced open with the help of a Winchester shell. Inside was nothing more than a single slip of paper.

That was the straw that finally broke the camel's back.

Wrong stage, wrong route – Better luck next time!

The mocking scrawl elicited a thunderous howl from Brazos. A leery smirk twisting the pursed lips of the guard was too much for the Kid.

'Think this is funny, mister?' he yelled, brandishing his hogleg under the audacious guard's moustached snout. It was clear even to Duke Miller that the Kid had lost control. A raging inferno blazed in his eyes. 'See how funny you think it is stokin' up the fires of Hell.'

Before Miller could stop him, three shots erupted from the muzzle of the Kid's revolver. And all three found their mark in the chest of the stunned guard. Buckling under the fierce impact, the man was dead before his body hit the ground.

It rolled beneath the hoofs of the stage team, causing the skittish horses to bolt, the wheels jerking over the supine corpse.

But the Kid was not finished.

'Now who's laughin'?' he burbled, pumping the remaining three shells into the mangled body. Then, without a word to the others, he swung his mount and spurred it viciously towards the distant mountains.

The others followed at a distance, each man wrapped in his own thoughts. Now the cat was well and truly amongst the pigeons. Gunplay had not been uncommon on previous raids. Shots had been fired, occasionally drawing blood but primarily to induce fear in their victims. So far it had worked. This was the first cold-blooded killing.

And of that, Lucky Brennan wanted no part. Especially when it had been one of his old friends who had been shot down.

With Lucky's stubbly face hidden behind a red bandanna, George Benson hadn't recognized his erstwhile partner from their days on the Utah run. Old George had been due for retirement next year. He'd always dreamed of heading out to California, buying a plot of land and growing orange trees. And now this.

With his own position in the gang tenuous, all that Lucky wanted was to quit while his hide was in one piece. To seek his fortune someplace else. It didn't matter where, just so long as he could escape the infamous reputation of a thieving outlaw. Not that he could blame the Blackhawks. If anything they had only acted as a catalyst to feed his obsession with seeking vengeance on the company.

But now things were different. A man had been killed and Will Brennan wanted no part of murder. He knew that once blood had been spilt, more would soon follow until the gang either bought a one-way ticket to boot hill, or met their Maker at the end of a rope.

That night, whilst the others slept, Will quietly collected his gear and disappeared into the night. Whether the gang would come after him once they discovered he had sneaked off, he neither knew nor cared. All he wanted was to put as much distance as possible between himself and a life on the run. Or a bullet in the back, whichever came first. He prayed that his reputation would not dog his flight north.

Will's intention was to hug the back trails, thus throwing any pursuit off the scent. Up through Black Dog Gap and across the Gila Valley, by the end of the third day he had reached his uncle's ranch close by Wickenburg.

Hailing from Kentucky, Hezekiah Brennan was brother to Will's father. He ran a small spread which specialized in taming wild horses and selling them to the army. Until the year before, he had run the place with his elder brother. But one careless moment had done for old Moses. All it took was a moment's distraction. That and a fatal kick from a loco stallion had split his head open, spilling raw brain matter all over the corral. Not a pretty sight, even for a seasoned veteran like Hez Brennan. Now he was forced to struggle on with help from a couple of hired hands.

Will knew he could trust his uncle when it came to outfoxing any pursuit whether by lawdogs or the Arizona Blackhawks. Even though the old guy had been awarded numerous commendations for bravery during the war against the North, he had left in a hurry following Lee's surrender at Appomatox.

Whether or not Captain Brennan was guilty of misappropriating company funds, Will had never enquired. He had no intention of so doing now. It was enough that his uncle agreed to misdirect any pursuit that might dog his trail.

So far he had succeeded, avoiding any contact with other human beings.

That is until now.

After four days of hard riding, he had entered the canyonlands of south-east Utah and come across this odd pair of . . what did they call themselves – archaeologists?

'Mr Brennan!'

'Eh?'

Jerked from his dreamy thoughts, Will shook himself back into the reality of his current situation. He peered across the scampering fire dancers into the soulful eyes of this strong-willed, determined girl. A right comely female there was no denying, he didn't quite know whether he was attracted to her, or repulsed. One thing was for sure, nobody could ignore her.

Most females he had come upon in his life were either caricatures of his mother – hard-working, loyal and dull. Or saloon temptresses – bawdy, colourful, ideal for a quick roll but nothing else. Jane Fanshaw was her own woman, that assessment had been obvious, even during the short time of their acquaintance. And woe betide any man who tried bending her to his will. Such a fella would end up hogtied and branded.

'I asked what you were doing out in this wild place,' she repeated a touch impatiently.

'Perhaps Mr Brennan doesn't welcome any interference into his personal circumstances, my dear,' interjected her father. 'After all, a man's business is his own affair.'

'That's OK, professor,' averred Will amiably. 'Just heading north is all. Hoping to make myself a fresh grubstake in Nevada. This here trail is a short cut that'll save me six days' travel. Sooner I reach Carson City, the sooner I can dig me some of that there yellow peril.'

Blake Fanshaw frowned quizzically.

'Gold!' hissed Will, his dark eyes taking on an iridescent gleam in the firelight. 'I hear tell it's the biggest strike since the California rush back in '49.'

'Has any gold ever been discovered round here?' enquired Blake, struggling to keep the tightness from his voice. Nonetheless it came out as a hoarse bark. He coughed to cover up the nervous inflection. Thankfully, the tall man appeared not to have noticed.

'Naw,' drawled Will, pulling on a cheroot. 'If that had been the case, word would have spread like a bad smell. And as you've found, there ain't nobody here 'ceptin' the three of us.' Will then tossed the smoking butt into the glowing embers of the fire and dropped a spare log on to keep it glowing through the night. 'If'n you don't object, folks,' he said, rising and stretching his arms, 'it's been an eventful day and I figure we could all do with a good night's sleep.'

In no time, a potent blend of nervous exhaustion coupled with the euphoria engendered by their discovery found the two archaeologists succumbing to the soporific embrace of the night. Only Will remained awake. His eyes gently absorbed the myriad of twinkling gems in the dark void overhead, whilst his mind attempted to make sense of the day's activities.

There needed something more to explain the presence of these two greenhorns in the Crawdaddy Breaks than they were prepared to divulge. Of that he was sure. Surreptitious glances, a tightness around the jaw, evasive answers to his queries – all pointed to a clandestine purpose underlying their presence.

But was that any business of his? Perhaps not. After all, didn't Lucky Will Brennan have his own nefarious reasons for choosing the Breaks trails.

After tossing things over with no solution forthcoming, a welcome visit from the sandman terminated his ruminations.

First light saw Will stoking the dying embers of the fire back to life and preparing breakfast. Another hour and the trio were heading back through the twisting labyrinth of canyons.

Sometime around midday they struck the main trail south.

'This is where I leave you good folks,' said Will, shaking the hands of the strange duo. The girl's touch sent a tingle up his arm, a feeling he had not experienced in a spell longer than he cared to recall. No shortage of female companionship had blunted his life on the owlhoot trail. A handsome guy with a pocketful of freshly lifted greenbacks always attracts the usual free-loaders. Not since his all too brief courtship of Ellie Summers had another woman affected him this way.

'We're much obliged for your assistance, young man. Perhaps we will meet again sometime.'

'Maybe,' murmured Will, his gaze held by the girl's

hypnotic allure. Keeping the notion buttoned up inside he added: 'I hope so.'

Blake's sincere assertion was echoed by his daughter. The assured easy-going manner of this tall dark-eyed paladin was something Jane Fanshaw had never come across previously. More used to the refined attributes characteristic of the eastern cities, she had discovered a basic, earthy persona striving to assert itself within her being. She now found herself inexorably drawn to Will Brennan and was sorry to see him depart.

'You will never know how much we appreciate all you've done for us, Will.'

That was the first time she had uttered his name in a casual, more personal manner. And it was most probably the last.

The grateful utterance mirrored in the limpid orbs was to be fixed in his mind long after the pair had disappeared from sight. And for days thereafter, as he trailed steadily north-west across the empty wilderness towards Carson City, a lonesome disposition began to take over his very being.

FOUR

IRON HORSE

'What did I tell yuh?' crowed Mace Cavanagh. The grin splitting his cadaverous mush revealed an irregular collection of yellowed stumps and cavities long past any form of dental repair. A stream of black tobacco-juice issued from the corner of his mouth. 'Knowed for damn sure that railroad was hereabouts.'

Lying side by side on a flat rock overlooking the dusty plain below, the four desperadoes surveyed the empty track stretching unbroken across their line of sight. Heading east as straight as a billiard cue and accompanied by a retinue of telegraph poles, the railroad disappeared over the horizon unhindered by any obstructions. But to the west and immediately below their vantage point it entered a rocky defile around a steep curve.

'This here cut's known as Delamar Gap,' announced Cavanagh with a nonchalant air. The old soldier was proud of his scouting prowess.

Miller immediately latched on to the possibilities. The train would have to slow down to take the bend. And that was their opportunity to jump it – literally! Shielding out

43

the sun's glare with his hamlike paws, Wild Cat posed the question Duke had in mind.

'How often do the trains run?'

'Three times a week,' replied Cavanagh confidently. It appeared that he was the only member of the gang with any knowledge of the railroad. 'Leastways, that was the case last time I rode it a coupla years back. And seein' as how today is Wednesday, we're in luck. Oughta pass through this cutting around noon.'

Miller ceremoniously opened a gold-plated pocket watch dangling from its chain. A rhythmic cadence punctuated the hot still air. Recently appropriated from an indignant banker during the course of their last hold-up, it was now his most prized possession.

The time read 10.07 in the forenoon.

He nodded sagely. 'Two hours and we pull our first train job.'

The announcement received mixed reactions.

As always, Wilson was sceptical. He hated change, even if the status quo meant starvation.

'Sure we can do a train, boss?' he questioned. The purple stain itched abominably, a sure sign of Wilson's uncertainty.

Brazos chided him with a mawkish click of the tongue. He was all for anything that was likely to improve his finances.

'With four of us it'll be a piece of piss,' he scoffed, aiming his next remark at the hulking brute beside him. 'Unless of course you ain't got the balls fer it, Cat.'

'You makin' out I'm gutless?' railed Wilson.

'He's in this just like the rest of us,' interrupted Miller sharply from behind his straggly black moustache, not wishing for any altercation between his men at this stage in the game. He hauled out the Smith & Wesson .44 and casually twirled the cylinder.

It was the latest nickel-plated '81 version and another acquisition from a generous benefactor. The whiskey drummer's reluctance to part with the prized revolver had earned its late owner a bloodied nose and matching pair of black eyes.

Sampling the poor dude's wares after netting an impoverished haul of only $30, the gang had released the team of horses. They had then proceeded to blast the coach to matchwood, leaving the three distraught passengers to hoof it back to the nearest settlement.

'Any objections?' The steely rasp brooked no rejoinder. Nevertheless, a craving to be top dog simmered just below the surface. Brazos hated taking orders. But he could wait. Miller was undisputed leader – for now. 'Well this is what we do,' he announced.

Once the details were firmly established, each member of the gang checked his own hardware. Miller had stressed that nothing should be left to chance, this being their initial foray into railroading hold-ups.

His orders were especially poignant for Wild Cat Wilson whose old Henry repeater had jammed at a crucial moment the previous week. Only the swift intervention of Miller exercising his right hand with the new Smith & Wesson had saved the hulking bear from an abrupt termination. In the event, it was the driver and guard who were left bleeding their lives away on the desert carpet, the gang having to flee once again empty-handed.

Even occupying a window seat with the sash fully lowered, Jane still felt like a broiled chicken. Unfastening her silk neckerchief, she wiped increasingly large beads of perspiration from her swanlike neck. Unfortunately, she and her father had been unable to secure seats on the shaded side

45

owing to the train being so crowded with passengers. Apparently there was an election of civic dignitaries being held at Beaver Creek – a rare opportunity for people to dress up and enjoy a party at the town's expense.

The six-hour train journey was not proving to be the most enjoyable of experiences, especially as the seats were unpadded.

'How much further?' she enquired testily of her father for the third time in twenty minutes.

'Another two hours should see us at Beaver Creek,' sighed Blake Fanshaw in a rather patronizing tone of voice. His advice was to 'Have a little patience, Jane. Just enjoy the view.'

'What view?' came back the curt response.

Poking her head through the window to allow the breeze to cool her heated brow, Jane found little comfort in the empty landscape through which the line passed. A sandy wasteland interspersed with clumps of withered sagebrush and hardy thorn rolled effortlessly away to the distant horizon. Even the rare appearance of a herd of buffalo failed to engender more than a terse sigh.

Pulling out the revered mearschaum, Blake ignored his daughter's blunt appraisal of the journey. He had heard it all before. A hot soak in a bathtub followed by a good meal would soon calm her petulance. Settling back, he relaxed into the gentle sway of the train, the steady thrum of wheel on rail lulling him into a light doze.

Most of the other passengers were likewise engaged.

It was the haunting wail of the loco whistle that brought him awake. We must be approaching Delamar Gap, he surmised sleepily. The conductor had informed him that the train had to slow down to take the sharp curve.

*

It was 11.45am.

'Time to go, boys,' announced Miller, giving his revolver and the Spencer carbine a final check. His next reminder was for Wild Cat Wilson.

Although the clumsy bruiser exuded a simplistic oafishness, when it came to handling explosives, he was the business. He always exhibited a catlike touch learned at first hand in the copper mines of Bisbee. And it was this source of Wilson's nickname that Duke Miller intended to exploit fully.

'Use the shotgun to blast open the express-car door, then set the dynamite against the safe like we planned.'

'Don't worry, boss,' replied Wilson knowingly. 'I won't goof up this time.' He knowingly patted the saddle-bags.

'You mean you hope you won't,' sneered Brazos.

Miller gave the Kid a reproachful glower before hurrying on.

'You should have no problem with the passengers,' he said, addressing Mace Cavanagh. Then offering a raised eyebrow, he said flatly, 'Anyone gits in yer way . . .'

'Bang! Bang!' The ageing *bandido* smirked, aiming a finger at Brazos. 'Gotcha, boss.'

Now that the time had arrived, a nervous tension gripped each member of the gang. Duke Miller idly toyed with the gold watch-chain, his jaw set firm. A nervous tic around the flickering eyes betrayed the brash nonchalance effected by the Brazos Kid. Sitting next to him and stiff as a month-old corpse, Wilson screwed his eyes down to slits studying the eastern prospect for signs of the train. Only Mace Cavanagh appeared to be unaffected by the imminent hold-up as he puffed casually on a cheroot.

A flight of squawking cactus wrens arrowing past overhead broke into Miller's cogitations. Another quick scan at his watch and the gang leader scrambled to his feet.

Shoulders square, there was a determined set to his leathery features.

'Time to go, boys,' he announced with excessive confidence. 'Hustle on down to where the track leaves the cutting. Soon as the train stops, git to work.' He eyed the grizzled assemblage, accepting their curt nods. 'If I ain't managed to stop it by then, you'll know I've failed. Then it's every man fer hisself.'

'Don't you be worryin', boss,' spoke up Wilson. 'Nothin' 'll go wrong.'

'It better not,' muttered the Kid, climbing on to his chestnut mare.

Soon the three riders were jigging their mounts down a narrow rock-strewn draw towards the open plain a half-mile distant, where the railway emerged from the cutting.

Miller crawled to the edge of the bluff and peered over to the track below. A jump of no more than six feet would land him on the locomotive fire-tender. That was providing the damn thing slowed down enough on the bend.

Then he heard it.

The howling lament of the approaching train.

Two minutes later, the monstrous locomotive with its forked cowcatcher trundled into view, a black cloud pouring from the bulbous smokestack. No wonder the Indians were scared to death of the legendary iron horse. But Miller's primary concern was its speed of approach to the cutting.

He gave a sigh of relief, preparing himself for the leap on to the tender. Keeping back from the edge to avoid being seen by the engineer, he sucked in a deep breath, took a quick peep, then launched himself into space.

Landing on the pile of logs sent a painful bolt jarring down Miller's spine. Thankfully the clatter went unheard.

Completely absorbed by the hiss and yammer of the huge steaming beast, both engineer and fireman had eyes only for the job in hand.

Throttling back the valves, the engineer gave another haul down on the whistle chain. Each loco boasted a uniquely individual tone achieved with the aid of wooden plugs hammered into the valve stem. This one emitted a mournful oscillating lament, a portent of what was about to befall the unfortunate crew.

Miller was more concerned that both crewmen kept their gaze forward as he struggled across the lumpy cargo of logs before scrambling down into the cab well.

'OK, boys,' he snapped firmly, long legs spread wide for balance. 'Pull this here hunk of iron to a stop at the end of the gap. And no funny business, you got that?' The wavering snout of the .44 emphasized his demand. The two men just stood there open-mouthed, hands clutching at the cab roof. 'So what yer waitin' on,' growled Miller prodding the engineer with the pistol. 'Haul back on them brakes.'

'Y-y-essir!' stammered the old guy, his long grey hair streaming back from beneath an oily cap. 'Anything you say, mister. Just keep that gun steady.' As he yanked down on the elongated brake lever, the engine huffed and balked, hot metal plates creaking and groaning at this unexpected demand.

But nothing appeared to happen. The engine maintained its speed.

Miller frowned. 'Why ain't this heap stoppin'?' he demanded, coarse features blossoming to a rich crimson as panic threatened to take hold.

'Give her time. The old gal needs careful coaxing,' said the engineer with a gentle twist on a valve wheel. 'Like all women, she don't take kindly to rough handling.'

'Just haul her ass up if'n yuh don't want a bellyful of lead.'

A harsh screeching of drive wheels locking on to the steel track almost jerked Miller off his feet. He clutched at the side panel of the cab for support. Seeing an opportunity to turn the tables on the bandit, the fireman grabbed up a shovel and made to crack it over the rannie's head.

Too late the foolhardy guy realized his mistake.

Lethal spurts of flame blasted twice in rapid succession from the Smith & Wesson. The dual crack echoed round the small cab as the two bullets ploughed into the fireman's chest. Blood spurted from the fatal wounds staining the greasy overalls, the force driving the unfortunate recipient back against the fire doors. Flesh sizzled like cooking bacon. But the unfortunate man was already dead.

Miller heaved open the cab door and pushed the body out.

'Any more heroics and you get the same,' he warned, screwing a belligerent expression into his face. The menacing threat was backed up by the lethal snout of the pistol jabbing at the fellow's ample midriff.

'Don't worry, mister,' spluttered the engineer, dragging hard on the brake lever, 'I'm due a nice pension this year. Ain't no way I'm about to jeopardize that.'

Miller took a quick look through the observation window. His men were already in place. Another half-minute and the locomotive shuddered to a halt.

'Climb down so's I can keep an eye on yuh,' ordered Miller. Then to his men he yelled: 'OK boys, the train's ours.'

'Yeeeehaaa!'

Wild Cat Wilson spurred his mount down the line to the express car behind the passenger coach, his large bay kicking up the gravelly bedding of the track. Drawing the double-barrelled shotgun from its saddle boot, a crazy grin etched the guy's ugly mush.

'Hey! You in there!' The gutteral shout to the guard was emphasized by the shotgun's steel-tipped butt hammering on the locked door. 'Stand aside if'n yuh don't want a hide fulla buckshot.' Purposefully, the doughty bruiser clawed back both hammers and let fly. A raucous blast smashed the door off its hinges.

At the same time, Mace Cavanagh and the Kid were clambering aboard the front entrance to the single passenger car. Hurriedly they pushed through into the plain interior.

Unlike the new Pullman Palace carriages that had been introduced on the main Union Pacific line, this one offered little comfort to the passengers. Bare and devoid of excess fripperies, it was intended purely for the conveyance of as many people as could be squeezed inside – just like sardines in a tin can.

Guns drawn and in full view, Cavanagh issued a calm yet resolute warning:

'Take it easy, folks, and nothin' will happen to yuh. Don't nobody move a muscle. This is a hold-up.'

Brazos was much more blunt, his lip curled to emphasize that they meant business.

'Yeh!' he snarled, twirling the Remington on his middle finger whilst trying to infuse a gutful of crazed zeal into his youthful harangue. 'Any one of you turkeys blinks outa line, he's buzzard-bait.'

The leery challenge met with a hostile if hushed murmuring. To accentuate the point, the Kid aimed his pistol at a lamp hanging from the carriage roof. It shattered into a thousand fragments spraying the surrounding passengers with oil and slivers of glass. Luckily it was unlit.

But the action served its purpose. Muttered imprecations instantly changed to gasps of fear, followed by a cowed silence.

'That's better,' smirked Brazos, swaggering along the centre aisle and waving the revolver with the sole intention to intimidate and arouse fear. The cringing passengers made him feel good.

With some attempt to calm and reassure, Cavanagh butted in, 'All we want is the contents of the strongbox in the express car. Then we'll leave you good people to continue your . . . '

He never finished the sentence. A huge explosion rocked the carriage. Dashing to the exit at the far end, Brazos hauled open the door and stared open-mouthed at what was left of the express car. The entire roof had disintegrated. Flames leapt from the mangled remains, black clouds of acrid smoke billowing skywards.

'What is it?' yelled Cavanagh relinquishing his normally placid demeanour.

'That stupid galoot's only gone and blown the damn blasted car to smithereens,' ranted Brazos, staggering back into the passenger car to escape the fierce heat. 'What we gonna do now?'

'Only thing we can do.' It was the firm yet gritty vocals of Duke Miller who had appeared in the doorway behind Cavanagh. 'Git what we can off'n these dudes then scarper *rapido* like.'

'Where's the engineer?' asked Cavanagh.

'Figured on playin' the hero, didn't he? So I had to put him to sleep.' He stressed the action by slamming the butt of his pistol against the door post.

Then he addressed the passengers.

'Now listen up, you people,' he said, accentuating the blunt remark with his .44. 'My two confederates will be coming down the aisle whilst I keep an eye on things. They will be more than happy to accept your valued contributions. All for a good cause naturally.'

'And that's us.' Brazos grinned inanely.

A quick glance informed Miller that no resistance would be offered, stunned as they were by the awesome destruction of the express car and its occupants. Then in a languid tone that certainly belied his feelings, Miller said quietly but with a definite hint of menace:

'I would advise you all to co-operate. Any resistance will be dealt with . . .' He paused deliberately, '. . . firmly.'

Brazos imparted his own inimitable addendum.

'What the boss means is, pay up or eat lead.' He cackled obscenely at his own crude wit.

Poking and threatening the distraught passengers, Brazos relieved them of anything of value whilst Duke Miller maintained a watchful eye over the proceedings. With Cavanagh checking the baggage, Brazos roughly searched the passengers paying careful attention to those well-dressed dudes who he assumed were carrying thick billfolds.

Scowling like a trapped cougar, the Kid was none too gentle with his frisking. He was livid about the large haul of greenbacks that had gone up in smoke. A cold flat glower screamed out a dire warning to all and sundry that he was just itching for some dude to give him the excuse to haul off. The fact that Wild Cat Wilson had come to an untimely end never even crossed his warped mind.

Towards the end of the carriage, Blake Fanshaw was becoming increasingly concerned that the chart marking the location of Montezuma's legacy was in imminent danger of being stolen. Judging by their diligent ransacking of the luggage, the gang clearly intended that the passengers pay heavily for the abortive raid. He shifted uneasily in his seat, a lean hand constantly pulling at the grey moustache.

One thing he had noticed, however, was that the females were receiving much less attention. It gave him an idea.

With this in mind, he slipped his right hand inside the buckskin jacket and grasped hold of the map. At the same time he leaned over whispering to Jane out the corner of his mouth.

'Conceal the map inside your undergarments. These men are only giving the women a cursory search.'

Intended as a clandestine exchange, Blake's nervous anxiety betrayed him. His jerky movements were like a red rag to a bull where Brazos was concerned. Thinking the old guy was drawing a concealed weapon, a rabid snarl erupted from the young gunman's twisted maw.

Without warning, the edgy silence was shattered by a harsh roar as the Remington spewed flame and hot lead at the archaeologist. Smoke and the acrid stench of cordite filled the air.

Slamming into Blake Fanshaw with the force of a charging buffalo, the deadly round punched him back into his seat. A dark stain rapidly spread across his chest. Not a sound escaped from his dry lips. Only a muffled sigh. Death was instantaneous. A scream of unsuppressed anguish broke forth from Jane's contorted features.

'Why did you shoot him?' she wailed jumping to her feet, 'He wasn't even armed.'

'Then what was he grabbin' at inside his jacket?' responded Brazos vehemently. He was anxious that panic amongst the other passengers didn't lead to any gallant gestures. Without waiting for a reply, he stuck his hand inside the jacket and encountered a thick wedge of papers.

'What's this?'

'Nothing,' croaked Jane, suddenly realizing her dilemma. 'It's nothing. Just some papers.'

'Musta been mighty important papers,' adjudged Brazos, fending the girl off. 'Let's just have a look see.' But with a school attendance record notable for its red absence marks, Brazos had never mastered the written word – other than those displayed on wanted dodgers. Yet even an illiterate gunslinger could recognize the main constituent. 'It's a map!' he yelped.

Too much experience of botched robberies had taught Duke Miller when to cut his losses. And this was just such a time. A time in fact to disappear into the wide blue yonder. A quizzical frown flickered across his face, causing his black eyebrows to meet. It was an unconscious habit but one that gave the gang boss a distinctively baleful expression. A sixth sense told him there was something more to those papers than met the eye.

He made a quick decision.

'We'll take the girl with us,' he rasped. 'Mace, you and the Kid take care of her. I have a feelin' this could be our lucky day.'

'We sure could use some,' muttered Cavanagh, taking hold of the girl's right arm.

'You leave me alone,' she cried sharply. ' I refuse to leave this train.'

Her spirited if futile resistance met with a curt response from the Kid. A sharp back-handed slap effectively cut short the girl's dissent.

But not without some reaction.

Balking at a lady in distress being manhandled by freebooters, a couple of the more enterprising male passengers jumped to their feet in protest. Two shots loosed off through the carriage roof from Miller's Smith & Wesson soon found them resuming their seats, cowed and embarrassed at their ineptitude.

'Anyone else feel like actin' the hero?'

No response.

Guns covering the rest of the passengers, the trio of outlaws with their terrified hostage backed down the centre aisle. Miller stayed in the doorway whilst the Brazos Kid gathered up the horses.

'One of us is gonna have to ride double,' he said, holding the reins for his *compadres*.

'Not since Wild Cat blew hisself into the next world,' parried Miller.

'Oh yeh.' The Kid smirked. 'I forgot. Now weren't that a darned stupid thing to go and do.'

Miller ignored the jibe. It was too late for misgivings now.

'OK, let's eat dust, boys,' he hollered, spurring his mount away from the hissing train, 'But afore we skidaddle, let's just remind these turkeys that they've been hit by the Arizona Blackhawks.'

Pistols belching loudly until they clicked empty, the gang made certain the passengers kept their heads well down. And that none of them forgot this day in a hurry. Not a window was left undamaged on this side of the carriage. Their bounties would be certain to increase after this fracas. A final yip and hurrahing echoed along the narrow cut as the gang urged their mounts up the shallow gradient.

Cresting a nearby ridge overlooking the smoking beast below, Miller reined his chestnut to a halt and pulled the ageing Spencer rifle from its equally worn scabbard. Often teased by the other gang members who preferred the 44.40 Winchester carbines, Miller had always sworn by a Spencer because of its reliability, ease of loading and range.

In this last attribute the weapon now showed its true worth.

Drawing a bead on the distant pot insulators holding the telegraph wires, he let fly three shots in rapid-fire mode. Each one found its mark, the released wires fluttering impotently in the light breeze.

'That'll give 'em somethin' to think on when the train fails to arrive at Beaver Creek on time.'

'You said it, boss,' averred Cavanagh, acknowledging the skilled shooting.

'Maybe you boys won't be so quick to run down the Spencer now,' replied Miller making no effort to conceal a proud grin.

As always, Brazo merely huffed.

'Give me a Winchester any day,' he scoffed, kicking his horse savagely down the back slope. Dragging Jane's mount behind, he almost tipped her out of the saddle. It didn't help that the distraught girl had her hands securely tied behind her back.

FIVE

NO PUSHOVER

It was another five hours before the train finally trundled into the junction at Beaver Creek. With the wires down, nobody knew what had happened. Passengers for the onward journey to Reno were threatening all manner of retribution for the delay. Faced with mutiny and suspecting the worst, the station master was in a near blind panic.

He was not to be disappointed.

Around five in the afternoon, with a lowering sun glinting on the locomotive's coal-oil headlamp, the badly bruised entourage wheezed and staggered into the station. Encased in a cloud of steam, it presented a sorry sight.

Luckily the bogies and chassis of the express car had escaped injury. Although, viewing the smouldering remnants, blackened and repugnant like a burnt steer's ribcage, luck could scarcely be an appropriate description.

It was a disaster of epic proportions.

The entire payroll for three herds of cattle had gone up in smoke. There would be hell to pay and no mistake. With sixty cowboys in town and no wages forthcoming, trouble with a capital T was brewing.

Jess Sinclair, the town marshal, shuddered at the thought. He nervously fingered the silvery tin star pinned to his leather vest. At twenty-eight he was on the young side for a lawman. Tall and spare with long blond hair worn in the fashion of his hero Wild Bill Hickok, a regulation drooping moustache made him look ten years older.

In other respects, Sinclair had moved with the times. He had acquired a Colt .45 Peacemaker rather than the '51 Navy model favoured by Wild Bill. The legendary lawman had been shot through the head by a saddle tramp called Jack McCall in a Deadwood saloon back in August of 1876. The killer was tried twice before suffering the ultimate penalty in Laramie the following year.

Since then, Sinclair had always sat with his back to a wall. And when involved in a poker-game he always folded if he ever held the 'dead man's hand' – a full house of aces and eights. Not that he was particularly superstitious but Jesse Sinclair didn't believe in pushing his luck that far.

He shook his head wearily, the untamed locks flapping beneath the brown Stetson. Sinclair's wife of three months was not going to be well pleased that her husband would very soon be facing down a hoard of angry cowpokes wanting their pay. Ever since he'd caught a bullet from a drunken cowpoke trying his luck at shooting down the moon, Abbie had urged him to surrender the marshal's badge in favour of the clerking position on offer in her father's general store.

But Jess enjoyed the job and it paid a heap more than store work. Even though he would never admit the notion to Abbie, he relished the excitement and prestige afforded to holders of the famed badge. So far, as luck or otherwise would have it, he had experienced little of the former.

In the five months since he'd been doing the job, serious disturbances had been few. Just the usual Saturday-night drunks: one occasion when he'd had a run-in with some rustlers, and a couple of land disputes. Jess was no slouch with a sixgun. But so far there had been little opportunity to test his prowess.

That situation was about to change. Elections were due and a train robbery would most assuredly prove whether or not he had the makings. And as the saying predicts – 'bad news travels fast'.

Within a half hour of the train arriving at Beaver Creek, the town was humming with the grim tidings. The numerous saloons along Main Street were soon throbbing with the strident babble of caustic comment. They were filled to capacity with cowhands sinking glasses of beer subsidized by their respective ramrods.

And news of the robbery was going down badly.

The first hint of trouble came from the Blue Peacock. One of the less salubrious establishments, it boasted an unenviable reputation for dubious high-stakes poker sessions, and soiled doves who supplied those all important 'extras'. It had been chosen by the Rocking Horse crew as their base of operations. And it was Big Jim Tyson who opened the proceedings. A first rate hand out on the range, a weakness for one too many drinks at the end of the trail transformed the reticent giant into a blustering hell-raiser capable of anything.

'What in hell's name is that god-awful racket,' he railed, slamming his pot down on to the bar top. A battered old piano and its accompanist in the far corner of the smoky room were the objects of his derision.

Somewhat less than melodic and pounded by a musician who was clearly tone deaf, the instrument clanged to an abrupt halt as a bottle crashed into the brass candelabra bolted to its lid. Lethal splinters showered the unfortunate player. Luckily it was only his battered derby that was shredded.

'There weren't no call for that,' wailed the cowering pianist from behind the object of Tyson's anger. 'Tain't my fault the durned thing needs tunin'.'

'Sounds more like a chorus of constipated cats,' roared Big Jim to the obvious delight of his cronies.

'You said it, Jim,' agreed a small bullet-faced cowboy. Lofty Cole nudged the big guy's elbow grinning widely. Unfortunately, the prod upended the whiskey chaser poised at Big Jim's fleshy lips, soaking his woollen shirt.

'S-sorry about that, Jim,' stammered the little fella. 'D-didn't mean n-no harm.'

Tyson glowered. His face reddened, contorting as the great black beard shook with fury. With a single jerk, he lifted the rotund fellow off his feet and sent him sliding the full length of the polished mahogany bar. A croaking yell issued from the mouth of the skidding cowboy as glasses and bottles scattered in all directions.

Hunched over his drink at the far end and minding his own business, one drinker just managed to side-step the rapidly approaching missile. But Will Brennan's drink, together with a bottle of the finest imported French cognac bought with his last silver dollar, disappeared along with the careering cowhand.

Cole hit the floor in a tangle of arms and legs. The stunned expression on Will's face was not reflected by the surrounding drinkers. Whooping loudly, they hollered rowdily at the unfortunate cowpoke rolling about under a table.

But Will Brennan saw nothing to laugh about. His hackles were well and truly raised. His dander was up and he was good and mad. A poisoned hiss broke from tightly clenched lips.

Normally a guy prone to thought and deliberation, Will's patience had been tested to the limit since arriving at Beaver Creek the day before. It had been his intention to rest up for a few days before continuing north to Carson City.

That was before his pack-mule had been stolen.

With no money to buy fresh supplies, he was up the creek without a paddle. No point reporting the theft to the local lawdog. Like as not he'd have a wanted flyer out on him. And the last place Will wanted to be right now was banged up in the hoosegow. The deck was sure stacked against him.

Peering at the stubbly apparition that stared back at him though the bar mirror, the notion that he had been labelled Lucky Will Brennan now seemed like a bad joke. He scoffed at the thought. All the indications now pointed to Will being forced back into his old profession.

He took a deep breath. One last bottle to bolster his nerve, then he'd break into one of the lock-up stores. That was the only way he was going to secure enough provisions to see him through to Carson City.

He took a sip of the fiery elixir, relishing the hot glow coursing through his body. If all went well, he could be on the trail and well away from this berg long before the alarm was raised. And with this latest hullabaloo over the train hold-up, that marshal would be kept busy for some time to come.

Now this!

Whipping out his revolver and with no thought to the consequences, Will snapped off a pair of quick shots. The roar of his .44 Frontier sliced through the din caused by Big Jim's paroxysm of temper. The big guy's black hat flew into the air, the second bullet flipping it into a shadowy recess.

And that was the moment Marshal Sinclair chose to make an appearance. Not having witnessed Tyson's outburst and the consequences to the offending piano, he assumed that Will Brennan was the cause of the fracas.

'Just drop that gun on the bar top, mister,' he said in a low yet firm manner. 'And keep your hands where I can see 'em.'

Will hesitated for a second.

'Don't make me put a hole in yuh,' came back the terse retort.

Doing as he was bid, Will swivelled his head to eyeball the speaker. Maybe a few years his junior, clad in a store-bought buckskin jacket, the lawman had ample firepower to back up his orders. Will had no intention of arguing with a double-barrelled Loomis shotgun, nor the .45 engraved Peacemaker in his other hand. Both pointed unwaveringly at his belly.

'Sure thing, marshal,' he replied slurring his words, 'but you got this all wrong. It was that ugly jigger what caused all the rumpus.'

'Who you callin' ugly?' roared Tyson pushing off the bar.

'Just look in that there mirror if yuh don't believe me,' retorted Will scornfully. Muffled chortles were soon stifled under the glaring snarl of the big cowpuncher.

'That's enough!' snapped the marshal, anxious to keep control of the situation. 'Seems to me like you was providin' all the gunplay.' He took in the bleary look and half-closed eyes of the stranger. Just another trigger-happy jerk who couldn't hold his drink.

'That's right, Marshal,' butted in Tyson with a furtive snigger. 'We was just havin' us a quiet drink when this jasper upped and started cuttin' loose with his hogleg.' The big guy looked to his *compadres* for support. 'Ain't that right, boys?'

'You said it, Jim,' from a cowboy to his right.

Quick nods from others. Lofty Cole had the good sense to keep his head down. Somebody handed Tyson his Stetson.

Poking a finger through the twin holes punched in the high crown, he crowed indignantly: 'Ruined a good hat an' all. Nearly took my head off with it.'

Not wishing to prolong the issue, Sinclair took a step back, gesturing for Will to precede him out of the batwings.

'A few days in the pokey will happen give you time to reconsider shootin' up a saloon in the future.'

'That's it, marshal. You jail him. Can't have these tearaways makin' trouble.' Ribald laughter erupted in support of Big Jim's sardonic remark. 'Us cowboys allus keep the peace.'

The mocking assertion was not lost on Sinclair but there was no law against free speech even though he suspected that another visit to the Blue Peacock was a virtual certainty at some point during the coming night.

'OK, boys,' hollered Tyson in his gruff bark once the marshal and his prisoner had departed. 'Everybody to the bar. Drinks all round.'

'And whose payin' for this lot then?' enquired the anxious bartender.

'Charge it to Walt Ryker next time he comes in,' yipped Tyson, referring to the trail boss. He banged his glass on the bar to emphasize the order. Big Jim Tyson knew his worth. And as leading point rider, he had earned a certain degree of status that the ramrod would acknowledge. 'The Rockin' Horse can foot the bill.'

More heehawing was followed by a mad scramble for the free booze.

Sitting in a corner ignoring the mêlée that had stirred up around them, a quartet of card-shifters sat hunched over their hands. All eyes were focused on the gradually swelling pot in the middle of the green baize.

But it was the dealer, a roving gambler by the name of Arkansas Pete Muldoon, who was showing signs of impatience. Slicked-down hair and a waxed moustache complemented the nifty blue serge suit. Fronted by a garish red vest, it was the sure sign of a professional at work. Pete had been working the saloons around Beaver Creek for the last three months since the rail line arrived.

'You gonna make a move, or fold?'

The curt enquiry was aimed at a well-dressed city slicker, a young tenderfoot who wasn't even wearing a gun. The gambler had every intention of fleecing the newcomer. Thus far in the game, he'd allowed the dude to gain confidence by winning a few hands. That state of affairs was about to end, which explained the gambler's vexation.

Unused to the sudden outbursts of violence that characterized frontier saloons, the young man had allowed his concentration to be diverted. The gambler's brusque query jolted him back to the situation in hand.

'Sorry about that, gentlemen,' he apologized, offering them a winning smile. 'My thoughts were elsewhere for the minute.'

'Now that you've seen fit to rejoin us, make your play!'

The disdainful rejoinder washed over the dark-haired player. He looked at his cards, then at each of the other players before replying. Beads of sweat and a twisted scowl on the pock-marked visage of Arkansas Pete only served to emphasize the dude's easy-going composure. Neither of the other two players seemed overly concerned. They had already folded. This was their regular Saturday venue. Some you won, some you lost.

Only the gambler was growing hot under the collar, and it showed.

'Well?' He almost spat out the exclamation.

A pregnant silence enveloped the small group.

'I call,' announced the greenhorn. 'Let's see what you're holding.'

With a smirk and a flourish, Pete laid down a full house of kings on nines, thinking he'd beaten the greenhorn easily.

'Whatcha think of that then?' he simpered, reaching for the pot, only to be met with a careless shake of a beringed digit in front of his hooked nose.

'Sorry about this,' sighed the dude, casually laying down his own hand. Puffing on a long cigar, he exhaled a plume of blue smoke before adding nonchalantly: 'In my experience a straight always beats a full house ... especially if it's a *royal* straight.'

Sharp intakes of breath preceded a gasp of surprise. Pete's jaw dropped, almost scraping on the sanded floor.

'Now if you don't mind, gents, I'm going to have to withdraw from the game,' continued the greenhorn, languidly reaching for the pile of greenbacks in the middle of the table.

'You can't do that,' snorted the gambler. His manicured hands clenched the edge of the table, the blanched knuckles stark against the dark-green baize.

'Why not?'

'You owe me the chance to get even.'

'What you really mean is you want the chance to clean me out.'

A hard edge had suddenly infected the dude's tone. He no longer conveyed the impression of being wet behind the ears. 'Think I haven't come across fourflushers like you before?'

Muldoon snarled. 'You callin' me a cheat?'

'Now why would I do that?' The younger man held the

66

gambler's acid glare. A lazy smile played across the handsome features. 'I won fair and square, didn't I, boys?' The others nodded uncertainly, anxious not to be drawn into any arguments that might result in gunplay.

Fixing the man opposite with a baleful glare, the gambler reached inside his velveteen jacket. 'Why you two bit . . .'

The hidden derringer never witnessed the light of day.

Muldoon froze. Without quite knowing how, he was staring down the barrel of a snub-nosed .38 Colt Lightning that had miraculously appeared in the young dude's hand. The small weapon had been hidden away inside a shoulder holster indicating that the 'tenderfoot' was clearly no pushover.

With a swiftness normally displayed by hunted rabbits, the other two players shuffled their chairs back to avoid any flying lead.

'Now, slow and easy, just lift that little beauty out and place it in the centre of the table,' ordered the young man, still eyeing the gambler with an unflinching stare, a fixed yet lethal smile pasted on to his smooth face.

Slowly Pete complied. His skull-like face was suffused a cherry red that indicated part anger, part embarrassment. 'You can pick it up at the marshal's office,' announced the blasé chameleon.

Gathering up his winnings, the young man backed off towards the door. The pistol was still levelled at Pete's midriff, just in case the slippery guy had other weapons secreted about his person. Only when he had left the drinking den did he relax.

He replaced the gun in its well-oiled holster and headed for the marshal's office two blocks down on the same side of the street. His polished boots echoed on the boardwalk. A couple of scabby mutts arguing over a discarded bone growled at the disturbance, then slunk away down an alley.

Knocking firmly on the reinforced oak door of the office, the stranger walked in after receiving an invitation. Jess Sinclair had just emerged from the cellblock at the rear. His right hand casually rested on the carved ivory butt of his Peacemaker.

'Can I help you, mister?' he asked, eyeing the newcomer suspiciously. Was it just coincidence that this dude had suddenly appeared as he was locking up another stranger?

'It's about that fellow you just arrested,' replied the dude, offering his hand. The marshal ignored the placatory gesture.

'What about him?' Sinclair tensed visibly, his knuckles whitening on the gun butt, shoulders hunched ready for trouble.

The young man read the signs immediately.

'Ease down there, Marshal,' he said lightly. The newcomer removed his hat and took a seat, an indication that he had no ulterior motive for the visit. 'I'm not after causing you any trouble. It's just that I saw exactly what happened in the saloon.'

'Oh yeh?'

'And you've got the wrong man.'

'How d'yuh figure that then?'

'I was in a game of cards over in the corner. I saw all the action. It was the big guy, the blustering cowboy who caused all the ruckus.' He went on to explain the sequence of events.

The marshal relaxed following the narration, then gave a perceptive nod.

'Big Jim Tyson.' He snorted derisively and reached for a tin mug on the pot-bellied stove. 'I mighta known it was him at the bottom of this. Fancy a cup?'

'Much obliged, Marshal.'

That was when the tenderfoot produced the small derringer from his pocket.

'What's that?' enquired Sinclair, stiffening a mite nervously.

'A gambler by the name of Arkansas Pete thought he could play me for a sucker,' explained the newcomer. 'The guy was a sore loser. He even accused me of cheating. I thought it best to relieve him of this before he used it on me. I may be new to these parts, but I've been around some.'

Sinclair handed him a tin mug of steaming Arbuckles.

'I reckon it's about time that shifty toad was encouraged to leave town. This story of yours is the third unsavoury report I've received about the table he runs.' He set his own mug on the stove and moved towards the rear door, rattling a large bunch of keys. 'Maybe I should let this guy out and go pay them cowboys a visit.'

A couple of minutes later a lean, somewhat dishevelled character appeared in the cellblock doorway ahead of the marshal. His eyes were red-rimmed and bloodshot, the gaunt face ashen and drawn. He leaned on a high-backed chair, swaying and threatening to collapse at any moment. A low moan escaped from his drooping mouth.

The young gambler hurried across the room and sat him down, holding out his coffee mug. 'Appears like you need this a sight more than me,' he said.

Will took the mug, a barely perceptible nod acknowledging the gesture. The strong brew appeared to infuse some life back into his stooped figure.

'You OK, fella?' enquired the marshal, offering an apology for the error. 'Sorry about the misunderstanding in the saloon. You're just lucky this gent happened to witness the whole caboodle. The last thing I need is a miscarriage of justice with the elections comin' up.'

Another groan escaped from Will Brennan's twisted mouth.

'That's the last time I overdo the hooch,' he murmured.

The lawman scowled. How many times had he heard that promise before!

'The gentleman appears to be in need of a good night's sleep,' suggested the gambler.

'Ain't got the necessary for a room,' moaned an inebriated Will Brennan. 'Can't yuh let me sleep it off in that cell back there, Marshal?'

'This ain't no hotel, mister.' Sinclair bristled indignantly. An apology was all this jasper was getting from him.

Will opened his mouth to protest with the added complaint that he had been robbed of his pack-mule. Just in time he clamped his wagging jaw tight shut. No sense in drawing unnecessary attention to himself. This fella might well have him leafing through wanted dodgers. And if his own mugshot popped up, that would really upset the apple-cart.

'Got somethin' else to say, mister?' enquired the marshal, noting Will's caustic frown.

'Only that I ain't got the readies for a hotel room,' he muttered.

'Then try the livery barn,' suggested Sinclair, becoming a mite exasperated.

'That's alright, marshal,' interrupted the tenderfoot. 'He can share my room over at the Drover's Cottage. It's got twin beds.'

Will eyed him askance.

'Seems like I'm beholden to you again, Mister. . . ?'

'The name's Ben, Ben Cassidy.'

Will stiffened. This dude was Jane Fanshaw's betrothed. Fortunately he was astute enough to keep his surprise hidden.

They shook hands.

Having settled the matter to his satisfaction, Sinclair ushered the unlikely pair out of the office and hitched up his gunbelt.

'This train robbery couldn't have come at a worse time, elections comin' up an' all,' he mumbled to himself. Then he set off back down the street.

In the distance rumbling thunder heralded the onset of a desert storm. As if to announce its imminent arrival, a few large drops bit deep into the hard-packed earth of the street. Jess Sinclair heaved a ponderous sigh. It was going to be a long night.

The marshal's final comment was a poignant reminder to Ben that he needed to get on over to the rail depot for more information on the hold-up.

SIX

BAD TIDINGS

'Where are you taking me?'

Apart from the intermittent creak of saddle leather and clatter of shod hoofs on rock, the question was received in silence. The query was repeated, this time aimed specifically at the man in black who appeared to be the leader of this unsightly gang of footpads.

'When my fiancé discovers you have kidnapped me and killed my father, he'll raise heaven and earth to see you all punished severely for this outrage.'

'I'm quakin' in my boots,' scoffed the Kid. 'No danged greenhorn is ever gonna flush out the Arizona Blackhawks. You tell her, boss.'

'That's right,' rasped Duke Miller acidly. 'Now quit yer squawkin', lady. I'll be askin' all the questions. But not 'til we find someplace to camp for the night.'

'And when might that be?' responded the girl curtly, her proud head held high.

'When I'm good an' ready.' Miller's retort was hard and brusque. He drew the single column of riders to a halt and turned to face the speaker. 'And if'n yuh don't button that

72

perty lip of yours, I'll have Brazos here strap yuh face down to that saddle.' An irregular display of yellowing teeth meant for a smile held the girl's challenging glower as the gang leader continued more forcefully, 'An' he ain't the gentleman what I am. That so, Kid?'

The young gunnie spat out an obscene leer, his lurid intentions all too obvious. *Pride cometh before a fall* – a poignant adage. Just in time, Jane decided that discretion was the more sensible option.

Once again the group settled down as they headed further into the desert wilderness.

This altercation was the first communication anyone had uttered since the gang had hot-footed away from the railroad following their abortive hold-up. Miller was still fuming. Would none of his schemes ever go right? A scowl emphasized the ugly scar beneath his right eye; the result of a misplaced bullet during a stagecoach robbery down Sonora way.

Then he thought about the map and its indications concerning the whereabouts of a stash of hidden gold. Maybe at long last a slice of good fortune was about to fall into his lap. And not before time.

It was another hour before Miller called a halt.

A tiny trickle of water issuing from the base of a craggy bluff sheltered by a belt of juniper offered the perfect camp.

Jane slid effortlessly out of the saddle. Grateful to stretch her legs and ease aching muscles, she received a numbing shock on peering into her looking glass. Hair that was normally groomed to perfection lay in rampant disarray, ribbons askew. Russet curls hung limp and bedraggled. She barely recognized the drawn face that stared back at her. Blotchy and streaked with dried tears, the erosive signs of strain and fatigue were all too evident.

Slumping down on to the hard ground, Jane buried her head in her hands.

Miller ignored her. His only concern was to determine what the all important chart would reveal. He removed it from his saddle-bag and pored avidly over the pictorial delineation.

Brazos was happy to let the others do the work. He sidled over to a rock and sat down, deftly rolling a smoke. A red tongue slid suggestively along the gummed strip, lustful eyes fastened on the girl's heaving frontage. He could wait, bide his time. But not for too long.

Out of the corner of her eye, Jane read the carnal signs. She shivered involuntarily, praying that Ben would find her before it was too late. He would be worried sick when the train finally arrived at Beaver Creek. And there was no way he would know which direction the kidnappers had taken.

The future looked decidedly bleak.

Meanwhile, Mace Cavanagh set to work gathering the makings for a fire to cook their supper. Soon the aroma of freshly brewed coffee and sizzling bacon percolated through Jane's distraught senses, reminding her that she was ravenous.

Darkness rapidly closed in on the isolated camp. The western tableau ablaze with a spirituous blend of flaming tints faded into the purple gloaming of approaching night. And with the heat of the day driven from her body, Jane shivered as the evening chill encased her.

Ever the thoughtful one, Mace offered the girl his blanket.

She took it without a word, although a grateful quiver of the full mouth was sufficient reward for an ageing dude like Cavanagh.

It was Brazos who couldn't keep his mouth shut.

'Allus the knight in shining armour, eh, Mace?' The

74

remark was heavily laced with venomous sarcasm. 'But yuh ain't got a chance with this catty minx.'

Cavanagh immediately took umbrage.

'Keep them juvenile comments to yourself, Kid.' The riposte hissed with menace. Mace Cavanagh might well be past his best, but there was no way some jumped-up punk was gonna mouth off about him in front of a lady.

Miller sensed the tension in the air.

'OK boys,' he said, 'just simmer down. We got things to work out and this gal has all the answers.' His next remark was aimed at Jane. 'Ain't yuh, girlie?'

His hawkish gaze carefully scanned the map indicating the location of Montezuma's legacy. 'Far as I can figure it, this secret cave is in a place called Johnson Canyon.' He looked to the girl for confirmation.

'That's just a name.' She shrugged, chewing on a piece of greasy fat back. 'All I know is we headed north from Kanab for about fifteen miles.'

'So you know the way?'

'No. I swear,' Jane averred fervently. 'My father and I were lost in the maze of canyons. It was only by luck that we escaped with our lives.'

'You're lyin',' snarled Brazos, grabbing her jacket. A harsh ripping of cloth accompanied the accusation.

A hint of panic crept into Jane's tremulous reply. She knew her very life hung in the balance where this gun-crazy kid was concerned.

'That's the truth,' she stressed, keeping her voice as even as possible. 'It was only pure chance that someone came along and saved us. Otherwise we would have been baked alive in that rocky wilderness.'

'And who was this good samaritan?' Brazos sneered.

'Just a traveller. He was heading north to Carson City.'

'Did he have a handle?' from Miller.

'Pardon?'

'A name, girl. What was this rannie called?' rapped the gang leader impatiently.

'Brennan.'

This startling piece of news was like a bomb exploding under the three outlaws. Instantly they were on their feet.

'*Lucky* Will Brennan?'

Jane nodded.

'Does he know about this treasure, then?'

'No,' announced Jane. 'My father only revealed that we were searching for ancient remains from the Aztec civilization.' She eyed Miller quizzically. 'So how do you know Mr Brennan?'

'That sneaky rat double-crossed us, then lit out. We been on his trail for the past month.' Brazos smiled. It was more like an ugly grimace. He drew his gun and twirled the cylinder. 'And now we know where that turkey's makin' fer.'

'That can wait,' rapped Miller. 'Gettin' our hands on this gold is more important. It could set us up for life. No more peerin' over our shoulders and dodgin' the law every day.'

Miller's black eyes gleamed at the thought. Then he turned to Cavanagh.

'Johnson Canyon,' he said thoughtfully. 'Ain't that up the Crawdaddy Breaks way, just over the Utah border?'

Cavanagh nodded.

'Best git some sleep then,' said Miller. He tossed a log on to the spluttering embers of the fire. 'We need an early start. The sooner we find this hidden loot, the sooner we'll be livin' on easy street.'

'That's music to my ears, boss.' Brazos smirked. 'And with a nice accommodatin' female to help me spend it, who could want for more.' The implication was obvious.

Jane shuddered at the thought.

Well aware of the Brazos Kid's lustful ways, Cavanagh ensured that his own bedroll separated the two. He might be following the owlhoot trail, but he still had standards where women were concerned. He had his old ma to thank for that. God rest her soul.

The Kid broke into his ruminations.

'Don't yuh trust me, Mace?'

With deliberate slowness, the older man withdrew his Winchester from its scabbard and levered a new cartridge into the barrel. Then he placed the carbine beside him on the blanket and lay down. No words passed between the two outlaws, but the meaning was abundantly clear.

It had been something of an ordeal for Ben Cassidy to manhandle his companion back to the hotel. Twice they had been forced to stop whilst the soused man emptied his guts down an alley. Figuring it would not be fitting to enter the hotel by the open front lobby, Cassidy had opted for the rear entry. His room was the first on the upper corridor at the top of the stairs inside the door.

After removing the guy's shabby boots and outer garments, he threw an eiderdown over the recumbent body, hoping that he had done the right thing. Grave doubts were creeping into his mind. As he left the room, locking it behind him, a raucous bout of snoring emanated from his new associate.

Ben hastened down the back stairs and hustled over to the railway depot. Realization that the train he had been expecting had been robbed and blown up was bad enough. But when he had learnt that someone had been shot and another kidnapped, a hollow feeling settled in his stomach. There was no reason to suppose that Jane and the professor were involved. But Ben knew his fiancée, and her equally obdurate father.

A black foreboding enveloped him.

Inside the small office, the bald station-master had his back to the door. He was hammering away at the morse key of the telegraph machine. Nothing was forthcoming. The line was completely dead. A chaotic mêlée of twisted wires spiralled upwards to the roof of the building and thence outside, where they attached themselves to a line of wooden poles.

'Danged road agents must have cut the wire.' He gave an exasperated snort. That's all he needed today when his wife had invited her mother round for dinner. The old battleaxe was a stickler when it came to meal-times. There would be hell to pay if he wasn't home on the chime of six. Arthur Honeydew was becoming increasingly frustrated.

'What information can you give me about the person who was shot?' enquired Ben.

'Have to send a dispatch rider over to the county seat at Cedar City,' mumbled the fraught official. A shiny film of sweat glistened atop the pink dome. 'This *would* have to happen in election week.'

Ben frowned. All anybody seemed bothered about in this greasy berg were the damn-fool elections.

'I want to know who has been shot and who has been kidnapped,' he repeated with forceful insistence. Still the man ignored him, huddled over his infernal contraption.

Then the penny dropped. The guy was wearing head-phones. Crossing the stuffy room in two strides, Ben jabbed an adamant digit into the man's back. The fellow almost leapt out of his skin with shock.

'You shouldn't oughta sneak up on a fella like that, mister,' he said having recovered his poise. 'Coulda given me heart failure.'

'Never mind that,' snapped Ben, swivelling the man's

chair round to face him. Then he repeated his question.

The station-master scratched at the balding pate, his smooth pink forehead creasing huffily. He looked askance at this intruder into his domain. 'This is railroad business,' he said officiously, peering down his nose. 'Why should I divulge any information to a complete stranger who's just wandered in off the street?'

Ben's patience was wearing thin. He grabbed the stout figure and heaved him out of the chair. Two buttons pinged as the sweat-stained shirt burst apart. The official's piggy eyes bulged, his flaccid jaw dropped.

'Now listen to me, you puffed-up little toad.'

Ben's nose was almost touching the other's twitching snout. Affecting a menacing touch of the theatrical, he spat out his demand quietly. 'If you wish to continue drawing your allocation of air, I suggest you answer my questions right now. Got that?' This last exclamation blasted into the guy's visage with the full fury of a rampant tornado.

Arthur Honeydew's belligerent manner instantly wilted.

'That's better,' continued Ben in a more conciliatory manner. He purposefully straightened the burbling guy's shirt and necktie. 'Now give me the details.'

'From what I can gather, having interviewed the other passengers,' began the station-master hesitantly, 'the dead man was accompanied by a much younger woman. It was she who was kidnapped.'

Almost before the frightened official had drawn breath, Ben feared the worst.

'Do you know them?' enquired Honeydew, having regained his composure.

'Maybe.'

'The gentleman's body has been taken to the mortuary, if you want to view it.'

'Were there any signs left as to which direction the outlaws took?' asked Ben in a daze.

'They just shot up the train and hightailed it into the desert. Nobody saw which way they went. Too busy keeping their heads down,' said Honeydew, anxious to bring this rather oppressive conversation to a close. 'Now, if there's nothing else, sir, I have a lot of work to do.' He busied himself with some papers on the scarred desk.

Ben just stood there, as if in a dream. The fat man gave him a wary look.

'One more thing,' said Ben. 'Where did the hold-up take place?'

'Delamar Gap. It's about fifty miles back up the track.'

Ben nodded idly, then left the telegraph office, leaving the huffy station-master to continue with his key tapping. Before he did anything else, Ben had to assure himself that the dead man was indeed Blake Fanshaw.

His visit to the town mortuary, located behind the doctor's surgery, was a melancholy and sobering experience that confirmed his worst fears.

Having learned the grim truth, Ben Cassidy returned to his hotel room, a bottle of bourbon under his arm. It wasn't only his unsavoury guest who had need of a liquid palliative to dull the aching void in his stomach.

With filled glass in hand, Ben's thoughts took a trip back to the previous summer.

Ever since he had first been introduced to Jane Fanshaw at the university ball in Chicago, Ben knew this was the girl for him. It was only because his own father had been called away on urgent business and could not attend the event that Ben had been reluctantly co-opted in his place.

He would have much rather been engaged in one of the numerous high-stakes poker schools that flourished in

Chicago's seedier quarter. Ben's weakness for the cards had been the principal reason his father had made him a working director of the company. To keep the young pup busy.

The ruse had only partially succeeded.

And this particular function, Ben had assumed, would be just as boring as all the others he had been forced to attend. How wrong his conjecture had proved to be.

As the honorary representative of Chicago's largest meat-packer, Ben had been seated at the top dinner table opposite the most beautiful thing he had ever set eyes on. Jane Fanshaw's self-assurance and witty repartee had hypnotized him from the beginning. Later that evening, they had danced the night away encased in a world all their own, unheeding of those around them. By the end of that first night, both knew that life would never be the same again.

Within three months they were engaged and making plans to marry.

Ben had been in Arizona to meet with some ranchers about a lucrative beef contract for the army. Knowing that Jane and her father were investigating a new discovery in the area, he had arranged to meet them at Beaver Creek.

Now this! His life destroyed in an instant.

An obscene grunting from the untidy heap on the other bed roused the business tycoon from his lethargic torpor. Cassidy wrinkled his nose, the mixture of alcoholic fumes and stale body odour made his stomach lurch.

Struggling out of his self-induced lethargy, Will Brennan sat up, leaning his back against the brass bedstead. A single eyelid prised itself open. Warily the eye took in the unfamiliar surroundings.

'Where am I?' he croaked, pushing back a stray lock of greasy brown hair. The echo of his own voice launched a staccato hammering of angry war drums in his head. Following a bout of sorrowful groaning from Will, the bleary peeper hesitated as it settled on to the other human being in the strange room.

Brennan gave a meaningful nod.

'Now I remember,' he slurred rubbing at his throbbing head. His flickering gaze settled on to the bottle clutched in the other's man's hand. 'You know what they say about the hair of the dog?'

Cassidy took a swig from the bottle, then set it aside out of reach.

'What I need is to get the hell out of this dump,' continued Will vehemently, lurching to his feet. But his rubbery legs were not yet ready and he collapsed back on to the bed.

'What you need is a gallon of black coffee.' Cassidy smirked. 'I'll order a pot sent up.'

A half-hour later, having sunk his fourth cup of the strongest Java, Will was beginning to feel something like his old self. If such a situation was possible after all that had happened in recent times.

But while he continued to tip the coffee down his gullet, his companion was well into the bottle of rye whiskey. A dour expression, becoming ever darker and more mystified, crinkled Ben Cassidy's normally handsome visage. With hardly more than a brace of stiff retorts uttered since the coffee had arrived, Ben was brooding on the import of the bleak tidings he had so recently received. His blank gaze, fixed on the cracked washhand basin, had not shifted one iota.

Curiosity eventually forced Will Brennan to address his good samaritan. He eyed the other man across the table.

'You were right about the drink,' he said, picking his words carefully. 'Ain't no solution to life's problems in the bottom of a glass.'

Silence.

Will tried again. 'Seems to me like you're better off talkin' things through.' He paused, taking another sip of coffee. 'And I got a mighty sympathetic ear.'

This time, the distraught man shifted his haunted gaze to stare at Will.

'What can you do, fella.' He snorted. It was a statement rather than a question. He reached again for the dwindling contents of the bottle. 'What can anybody do.' This time it was Will who moved the tantalizing elixir out of reach.

'Maybe nothin'. Maybe offer some help. I won't know unless you tell me.'

'Oh, what the heck!'

Then it all came out. The archaeology expedition; Ben's own business meeting and intended rendezvous with the Fanshaws; his penchant for gambling and most recent fracas in the saloon. But it was the recounting of the traumatic events of the rail hold-up that caused most upset.

Will probed away like a newly qualified surgeon. With a mixture of gentle persuasion and terse cajoling, he finally managed to extract the grisly details from the tormented soul of his new associate.

'So what did these desperadoes look like?' was his final enquiry.

Ben's ruddy complexion darkened perceptibly. His eyes shrunk to thin slits, the square jaw tightened. As he gripped the table, his reply literally hissed out.

'According to the station master, the leader was a big dude dressed all in black. Oldish fella in his forties with a southern accent.' He failed to note the sudden tension in his companion's manner, the lips drawn back into a chilling grimace. 'Another of the outlaws, a cocky young sprig—'

'The Brazos Kid!' interrupted Will in a flat, barely audible whisper.

Cassidy continued as if he hadn't heard. '. . . even told the passengers the name of the gang that was robbing them. They must rank as the wildest, most despicable bunch of desperadoes this side of the Mississippi. If I ever get my hands on them lowdown skunks—'

'The Arizona Blackhawks!'

This time, Will's interruption drew rein on Cassidy's harangue. Ben stared wide-eyed at the other man.

'You know these bastards, then?'

Will ignored the question.

'I said do you—'

'I know what you said, mister.'

'Well?'

Will hesitated. He reached purposefully for the whiskey bottle, his angular features thoughtful and resolute as he took a deep slug of the heady brew.

'Rode with them a while back,' he said at last.

'What?' Cassidy lumbered to his feet. He stepped back as if to distance himself from this link with his fiancée's kidnappers.

'Broke away from 'em when they started to killin' folks,' continued Will, unfazed. 'By tryin' to take on a train, it sure looks like they figured on uppin' the stakes.' Noting his companion's questioning look, he elucidated. 'Duke Miller, the leader, never did more than small-town banks and stage coaches. It will have been Mace Cavanagh who persuaded him to go for a train hold-up. Just typical of that two-bit outfit that they made a mess of it.'

'Well, that's no consolation to Jane,' replied a despondent Ben Cassidy injecting a note of bitterness into the riposte. 'And with Blake dead, she must be suffering shamefully.'

This time it was Will's turn to jerk upright.

'You talkin' about Blake and Jane Fanshaw?'

Ben gave a puzzled nod.

'I came across them whilst I was passin' through the Crawdaddy Breaks,' Will explained.

At Ben's urging he went on to outline the events of the meeting, how the archaeologists had become lost amid the maze of canyons and his part in their rescue from the mountain lion.

'Last I saw of them was after we hit the main trail back to Kanab. They headed south for the railhead, and I turned west for Carson City intending to find me a grub stake on the new bonanza up that way.' After a reflective pause he made the rueful comment. 'That sure is some feisty gal you've gotten involved with.'

'That was what attracted me in the first place, that and her being the most beautiful woman I ever set eyes on.'

Will silently agreed.

'And now she's in the hands of a vicious gang of outlaws.' Cassidy's voice crackled with pent-up emotion, his grey eyes misted over. The struggle to maintain his composure proved almost too much. To hide his discomfort, the Easterner quickly hurried on. 'How come you was in that neck of the woods anyway if they had wandered so far off the beaten track?'

'I reckoned that bunch of losers would come after me when they discovered I'd lit out. That's why I avoided the main trails.'

Following these revelations both men were sorely in need of liquid sustenance. Ben went down to the bar for a fresh bottle. Over the next couple of hours, this unlikely pair of confederates, thrown together by a bizarre set of circumstances, determined that they would join forces and go after the outlaw gang.

Will hoped to turn the tables on his erstwhile *compadres* and maybe claim some much needed bounty lucre by turning them in. Dead or alive, he wasn't fussed any more. He tried without success to persuade himself that this was his only motive. But a vision of Jane Fanshaw's sylphlike features surrounded by a cascade of titian hair kept impinging on to his senses.

Having thrashed out the details of their plans for the following day, both men fell asleep assisted by a liberal helping of the amber nectar. The image of his beloved fiancée in the grubby hands of desperate outlaws eventually pursued Ben Cassidy into the arms of Morpheus.

With similar pictures haunting Will Brennan's subconscious, the future might well hold some unexpected surprises.

SEVEN

TRAPPER DAN

Before the deep indigo of night had faded with the coming dawn, Miller was badgering the untidy group of travellers into wakefulness. With characteristic sluggishness, the outlaws broke camp. Following a desultory breakfast of hard tack and black coffee, they picked their way in single file along the narrow trail. Already the false dawn was bathing the western fringes of the mountains in a pale glow.

By mid morning the deep azure of the sky had turned to a dull grey, with bunched stacks of murky cumulus heralding the arrival of a thunderstorm. Above the distant mountain peaks bright flashes lit up the darkening sky. A booming rumble of thunder followed soon after.

The rains broke just after midday. Driven down the canyon by a relentless desert wind, the force of the blast almost unseated Jane. She clung desperately to her mount. Within minutes, they were all soaked to the skin.

By late afternoon, the constant saturation was beginning to take its toll. Jane in particular was suffering from the incessant cold effected by the buffeting wind. Mace Cavanagh had offered the girl his slicker to help alleviate the biting chill, a chivalrous action that caused the Kid much amusement.

'Keep yer eyes pealed for some shelter,' shouted Miller from the front without turning his head.

But it was the eagle-eyed Mace Cavanagh who announced the news they all heartily welcomed. He pointed a gloved hand at a small log cabin secreted beneath an overhang of rock one hundred yards off the trail. Another minute and they would have passed it by.

After they had secured their horses Miller shouldered his way through the plank doorway into the single room. It was empty, but clearly inhabited by some *hombre* judging by the personal accoutrements scattered about. Cavanagh quickly assembled the makings for a fire in the large stone grate. Soon, wisps of steam were rising from their wet garments.

Apart from the door, there was only one other aperture, a window covered by deerskin. Various other skins were pinned up on the rough log walls together with a couple of sets of fine caribou antlers. On one side of the door was a single bed covered with a thick brown bearskin. A chest of drawers occupied one wall, a few cheap trinkets were spread over its once polished surface. The only other furniture was a homemade table and chair. In the far corner behind the door lay a stack of furs.

Occupying pride of place on the mantleshelf was a framed picture of a man of about forty years posing stiffly in Sunday best behind a much younger Indian girl. His left hand rested affectionately on her shoulder. Its sepia tones were those favoured by the photographic studios that were burgeoning in all the main towns.

Since the sitters had perforce to remain still for long minutes at a time to avoid a blurred image, the result was often a wooden starchy depiction of their poses. Even so, Jane couldn't help noticing the love that these two people clearly had for each other. They must be the occupants of the cabin.

A single tear traced its delicate course down her ashen cheek. It reminded her of her own precarious situation. Would she ever see Ben again?

But such thoughts had no place here. Only the strong-willed, gritty resolve handed down from her recently departed father prevented the distraught girl from breaking down. She was determined that these desperadoes would not break her spirit.

It was Cavanagh who disturbed her dreamy yet insistent reflections.

'The galoot what lives here must be a trapper,' he observed, peering around the dimly lit room.

Miller nodded and applied a lighted match to an oil-lamp. Then he smiled mirthlessly, settling himself into the comfort of a padded rocking-chair.

'And ain't he gonna git a surprise when he returns!'

'Too right, boss,' chortled the Kid.

'See if there's any food about.' Miller's curt order was aimed at the girl.

'Yeh,' snorted Brazos with a surly grin. 'And make it quick, I'm hungry.'

'You get out on that porch an' keep yer eyes peeled,' snapped Miller to the Kid.

'Why me?' whinged the Kid.

' 'Cos I said so. Now git!'

Grumbling under his breath, the Kid nevertheless obeyed.

After rummaging round the cupboards in the shack,

89

Jane found some potatoes, a sack of beans and some tins of stewing meat. She set to work with vigour. Not having eaten properly since the previous morning, before she and her father had left Kanab, Jane was herself famished. Mace Cavanagh's culinary expertise might well suit desperadoes on the run. But not a girl used to dining in the finest restaurants.

That was when a scuffling in the log and brushwood roof above her head brought a startled gasp from the girl's lips. This blossomed into a full-throated scream as two giant-sized rats fell through a hole on to the floor.

On his feet in an instant, Miller grabbed at his holstered revolver, fanning the hammer. The crash of the six charges merged into a single blast as he emptied the contents into the loathsome creatures. Blue smoke filled the cabin, the ear-splitting noise reverberating round the tiny room.

Idly leaning against the rough log walls on the outside porch, the Kid almost parted company with his skin when the gunfire erupted. Recovering his composure he dived through the doorway, gun in hand, a panic-stricken croak in his voice.

'What happened? Why all the shootin'?'

Miller couldn't conceal a biting chuckle. 'Just makin' sure you don't go hungry, Kid, that's all,' he announced with a nonchalant shrug.

'Eh?'

'Yer supper.' He pointed the barrel of his .44 at the twitching carcasses on the dirt floor.

Cavanagh and Miller both howled with laughter, tears rolling down their cheeks. Even Jane couldn't resist a brief smile on witnessing the stunned expression on the Kid's face. His twitching jaw almost hit the floor. Never one to appreciate jokes at his expense, for once the tough Brazos

Kid was lost for words. To hide his embarrassment, he slammed out of the cabin in a surly huff.

The grim atmosphere, temporarily lifted, soon returned as Jane remembered where she was and what was likely to happen once the outlaws found the hoard. Desperately trying to throw off the reminders of her dire predicament, Jane forced herself to think positively. After all, wasn't she her father's daughter – the resolute assistant, capable and efficient, who had insisted on accompanying him in search of Montezuma's lost treasure.

Now, only the thought of Ben Cassidy leaving no stone unturned in his pursuit of the gang prevented all this feisty pretence crumbling to dust. It was a notion she had to cling to if her sanity was to be preserved intact.

A regular drumming on the wooden roof of the old cabin was a reminder that whilst the storm lasted she would be cooped up in the smelly hovel with this unsavoury bunch of ne'er-do-wells.

With a heavy sigh, she spooned out a bowl of stew and handed it to Duke Miller. Yes indeed, it was going to be a long night.

It was already well past sun-up when Miller surfaced. Jane had been up for half an hour and was heating beans and fried potatoes over the fire. Miller shrugged off a blanket and stretched cramped muscles.

'That sure smells good,' he said, belching loudly. 'And I could use a cup of that there coffee.'

Wrinkling her pert nose in disgust, Jane stifled a reply as she handed the gang boss a tin cup of the steaming brew. At least he'd allowed her to sleep in the only bed the cabin possessed. Not that sleep had come easy. With her mind in such a turmoil whilst trying to keep warm beneath the smelly blanket, Jane had been only too pleased when the first hint of dawn had filtered through the window.

'Sounds like it's stopped rainin',' remarked Miller, raising the cup to his thin lips.

He never got to taste the black liquid.

At that moment, the door crashed open and a hunched figure appeared in the open space. Silhouetted against the pale lilac of early morn, the wild apparition was bearded and clad in buckskins. Long straggly hair flapping in the wind like a torn flag gave the intruder a sub-human appearance, as if he had grown out of the brutal landscape from which he had suddenly appeared.

All very well, but it was the black barrel of an army Remington at full cock that drew the bulging peepers of Duke Miller. This was no phantom from the stone-age.

'Don't think on it, pilgrim,' snarled the bristling interloper. The black orbs gleaming in the dim light cast by the fire instantly took in the scene, and Miller's hand straying towards his own revolver.

The gang leader froze. The commotion had also brought Cavanagh to full wakefulness. He sat up, staring goggle-eyed at the bizarre figure in the doorway.

'Who in tarnation are you?' he asked.

'Seein' as how this is my cabin, I'll be askin' the questions,' retorted the wild man gruffly, emphasizing his claim with the wagging sixgun. 'Now what you a doin' of on my property?'

Miller had no hesitation in voicing his response.

'We're prospectors,' he replied, quickly recovering his poise. 'Came across this cabin last night and found it empty. I figured the owner wouldn't object if we took shelter from the storm. Surely you ain't begrudgin' us refuge.' Miller's tone was the epitome of the honest traveller.

The man looked from one to other, his black eyes glittering angrily from beneath grizzled brows. A questioning frown scored his brow when his gaze came to rest on the girl.

It was impossible for Jane to guess at the man's thoughts under the heavy beard. She was debating with herself whether to appeal for his help. Would he offer the assistance she needed in returning to Beaver Creek? Or was he just another desperado on the make?

Too late; the decision was abruptly made for her.

The Brazos Kid, who had slumped down on a heap of furs behind the door following a heavy night on the bottle, suddenly leapt to his feet. Ramming his shoulder against the open door, he sent the intruder lurching into a pile of iron traps.

The others were not slow in taking advantage of this change in fortunes.

Miller grabbed the fallen Remington whilst Cavanagh and Brazos wrestled the hapless captive on to the dirt floor. He squirmed and cursed volubly at the trespassers until a solid cuff to the jaw from Cavanagh brought his futile struggles to an abrupt halt.

Brazos scooped a cup of water from the butt and tossed it the guy's face. Glazed eyes slowly opened as the grisly visitor attempted to focus in the dim light. He groaned, more in exasperation at being suckered than from any pain.

'Now it's my turn to ask the questions, mister,' snarled Miller, his knee firmly pressed into the other's back while he jabbed the snout of the Remington into its owner's hairy ear. 'What's yer name? And what might you be doin' in this god-forsaken wilderness?'

The man gasped, struggling to draw air into his lungs.

'Let me up an' I'll tell yer,' he panted. Miller considered, then gave a curt nod. The other two hustled their catch to his feet and pushed him unceremoniously down on to a chair. Three deadly gun barrels were enough to banish any thoughts of retaliation from the man's head.

'Name's Daniel Heggerty,' he said after drawing breath. 'Some folks call me Trapper. I been huntin' in these parts fer nigh on ten years.'

'Trapper Dan?' exclaimed Cavanagh.

'The very same.'

'You know this turkey?' enquired Miller.

'Only by reputation,' murmured Cavanagh, his voice almost deferential. 'This guy is famous back where I come from. Last of the great beaver-trappers.'

'Built this cabin when I moved over from the Utah canyonlands after my wife died of the fever. Prospecting didn't seem to appeal much after that. And I never had much luck with the diggings anyway. Hardly made enough to even give her a decent funeral.' His deep-set eyes misted over, but only for a brief instant. 'That's when I found that trapping for furs was a steadier means of earning a living. Not like it used to be in the old days of the rendezvous, mind. But there's still plenty to catch if you know where to look.'

'Is this your wife?'

It was Jane who posed the delicate question, the old picture in her hand.

Heggerty nodded, his eyes once again filling up.

'There ain't a day goes by when I don't think of her,' he said, gently taking hold of the scarred frame and gazing wistfully at the image of a dark-haired smiling young Navajo squaw.

'Enough of this garbage,' Brazos snorted. 'I say we shoot the bastard now and be on our way.' The click of his

94

revolver to full cock accentuated the resolve etched across his surly features.

Miller quickly butted in.

'I give the orders here. Now haul back on that hogleg.' Brazos grunted disdainfully then slowly complied.

'You sayin' that you was a prospector in Utah?' asked Miller, addressing his query to the trapper.

'That's it.'

'Ever worked the Crawdaddy Breaks?'

'Know 'em like the back of my hand.'

Miller stood up, went across to the fire and poured himself a cup of coffee. Cavanagh could sense that the gang leader was hatching up some new scheme.

'What yuh got in mind, boss?' he asked casually.

Duke Miller was new to this part of the country. Ever since they had lit out following the abortive train robbery, he had displayed all the panache and confidence expected from the leader of the Arizona Blackhawks. No hesitancy as to the direction in which they should ride the trails, he had led from the front, the others following like sheep.

But all he knew for certain was that the Crawdaddy Breaks lay to the east, over the Utah border. The truth of the matter was, he was lost. And now the time had arrived where he had to admit the truth.

But how to broach the matter?

He didn't want to lose face. Mace Cavanagh would stick by him. But the Kid? A belligerent hothead, lethal with a shooter, he could easily take it into his head that Miller was a has-been, a liability, and that he, the Brazos Kid, should be leader.

Miller turned away, his back to the others so none could witness the disturbed expression of his ashen face – a tightness about the jaw, the hunted frown. Resolutely, he turned to face them, shoulders set firmly. Only a slight nervous tic of the eyelid betrayed any lack of self-assurance that he might be feeling. He took a sip of the strong sweet coffee to calm his jangling nerves.

Nobody suspected Miller's uneasiness. All they witnessed was a tough rannie capable of dealing out lead and much more when the need arose. And now was the time to play out that role. This jasper offered a perfect way out of his dilemma.

It took much of the following day for Will Brennan to purchase the supplies they would need and a pack-mule to carry them. Financed by Cassidy, who had paid an early call to the bank, Will was now legally able to acquire the best of everything. First stop was the barber's shop for a haircut and shave followed by that most enjoyable of all luxuries, a long soak in a hot tub.

Back in the hotel room, Cassidy was chafing at the bit. It was mid-afternoon before Will returned to the hotel.

'Where the heck have you been?' He bridled. 'We should have been on the trail hours ago.'

'Seein as how you're payin,' replied a smiling Will Brennan, preening himself in the long mirror attached to the wardrobe door, 'I figured you would object to a part-ner what smelt like a pig's midden.'

Cassidy blustered some but let it pass.

'So are we all set to go now?' he pressed, anxious to be off.

'Everything is outside, ready and waitin'.'

'I'll pay the hotel bill, then we can be off. There's still a good four hours' daylight left.'

'Sure thing, *pard*.' Will gave an exaggerated salute, emphasizing his reply to let his new partner know they were equals in this enterprise. He packed his personal effects into a pair of scuffed leather saddle-bags, slung them carelessly over his shoulder and strutted from the room.

Ten minutes later they were heading down the dusty main street of Beaver Creek, Will leading the stroppy pack-mule on a tight rein. Another hour and the small rail junction had disappeared from view as they topped a rise heading east towards the distant jagged peaks that heralded the onset of the canyonlands proper.

'Ever come across a place called Johnson Canyon?' enquired Miller tentatively, eyeing the trapper from beneath a lowered brow. He had tried to make the query as casual as possible.

But Trapper Dan was no fool. He uttered a raucous guffaw, slapping his thigh and stamping a knee-high moccasin. 'I knew it! Soon as saw yuh.' The jolly demeanour continued as Heggerty poked a grubby finger at the gang leader. He chuckled gleefully, 'You guys are after the legendary treasure of Montezuma, ain't yuh?'

Nobody spoke. They were too stunned.

'Well, ain't yuh? No use denyin' it. I know that's what yer after. Think I haven't heard about it, all those years scrabbling around in the canyonlands?' He hurried on, a bitter inflection now tinging the diatribe. The black eyes seemed to gleam as Trapper Dan stared at the dancing flames in the stone hearth.

'That's what brought me to the Crawdaddy Breaks in the first place. When I was over in California back in . . .' The old dude thought for a minute, scratching at his greasy pate. '. . . Musta been afore that first discovery at Sutter's Mill on the American River. Stories were circulatin' about a fabulous hoard left by the Aztec king

Montezuma hundreds of years back. I spent twenty years searchin' for that treasure. And all fer what.' He hawked a gob of phlegm into the grate. 'Peanuts!'

Then Heggerty stood up and crossed to where Jane was still clutching the painting. He gently took it from her and stared at the faded image. Tears filled his eyes. 'And a dead woman.'

'How did it happen?' asked Jane quietly.

'Greed and obsession, miss,' replied the trapper vehemently. 'I should have gotten her to a doctor soon as the fever hit. But no. The great Dan Heggerty had to keep diggin'. Always thinkin' he was about to discover the big one, the fabled El Dorado.'

'Ah!' interrupted the Kid, 'but we got a map.'

'Thank I ain't had a map?' snapped Heggerty. 'Loads of 'em. And all worthless.'

'But this one's genuine. The real thing,' added Miller forcefully.

'Aren't they all.'

'He's right. Mr Heggerty.' Jane's serene demeanour halted the trapper's melancholy reflections. He peered at her keenly, willing her to continue. 'My father was an eminent archaeologist from Chicago who spent his whole life studying the Aztec culture and its history. This was to be the crowning glory of his career . . .' She paused, pointedly surveying each gang member in turn. '. . . until he was shot down in cold blood by these . . . gentlemen!' This last word she spat out.

'So that's it, eh?' said the trapper slowly. 'The little lady here's been kidnapped to lead you fellers to the treasure. And not one of you ragtails knows the way. You've gotten yourselves lost. Seems like I got the whip hand then, don't it? Shoot me and you ain't gonna find anythin'. Except that is if'n yer after a lonely grave.'

With that, Heggerty burst out laughing. But the hilarity he found in their situation failed to impress the gang.

'Shut him up, will yuh,' bellowed the Kid at the room in general, 'before I do somethin' I might regret.' His exasperated riposte was tinged with a measure of hesitancy. Even he recognized that Trapper Dan Heggerty did indeed hold the whip hand if they were ever going to find this so-called treasure.

Eventually simmering down from his mirth, Heggerty spoke to a somewhat deflated Duke Miller.

'Let me see this here map so's I can figure out the situation.'

Miller extracted the sheet from his saddle-bag and handed it to the trapper.

For some minutes Heggerty studied the spidery hand that had sketched out the map, muttering various unintelligible imprecations to himself.

'Well?' spoke up Miller, 'You know this spot then?'

'Maybe.'

But Brazos had had enough. 'This varmint's just playin' with us,' he snarled drawing his pistol. 'He don't know nothin'. I say we blast him and get the hell out of here back to Arizona.'

Heggerty cut in quickly, recognizing that the Kid was mean and deadly. A young killer capable of drilling him without a moment's hesitation.

'Now did I say I didn't know? Of course I do. Been down that canyon many times. I just never searched in the right place. That's all.'

'How long will it take us to get there?' spoke up Cavanagh.

'Four, possibly five days.' Then he held up a cautionary hand. 'But let's not be so hasty. I figure you fellers owe me for some bed an' board.'

Miller puffed out a frustrated sigh. 'How much?'

The trapper gave an exaggerated tilt of the head, making out he was thinking hard.

'Let's just say I want an equal share in all we find,' he said, after a moment.

'You thievin' son-of-a-bitch,' ranted Brazos. 'We do all the graft and you take the biscuit.'

'That's my offer. Take it or leave it.'

'What d'yuh reckon, Mace?' said Miller, knowing that his older partner was no slouch when it came to sussing out the best deal.

'In my view, we ain't got much choice,' he replied. 'Gun this rannie down and we're back to square one. At least this way, we all have a chance at makin' it rich.'

'OK, mister,' Miller told the trapper. 'You got yourself a deal. But one false move—'

'Don't worry, pard. I know when I'm well off.'

'Then let's get packed up and on the trail.'

Within the hour, the five riders had left the lonely cabin and were heading east in single file towards the mountain fastness of southern Utah. Heggerty had taken the lead followed by the girl. In the rear, Brazos simmered and seethed, his furrowed brow becoming ever more pronounced. He hated anyone getting the better of him. If looks could kill, Trapper Dan would have been buzzard bait by now.

He drew hard on the thin quirley then threw the butt away. With a vicious dig of his silver Mexican spurs, he rowelled his mount up beside that of Duke Miller.

'You shouldn't oughta have let that guy take over, boss.'

Miller gave him a leery smile, then leaned towards his young partner offering a low whisper.

'Don't worry, Brazos. Once he leads us to the loot, you

100

can let that iron of yours do the talkin'.'

The Kid responded with an icy grin and slapped the bone handle of his revolver. Miller visibly relaxed. Once again, he felt in charge, confident that his authority was still intact.

A platoon of orange dust devils spiralled across their path. Patrolling in a regulated formation, they reminded Miller that any slackening of discipline within his own ranks and the Kid would take full advantage.

EIGHT

WAR PAINT

Stalking Bear drew his pony to a halt on the edge of a deep precipice overlooking one of the innumerable ravines that characterized this part of south-west Utah. This was the Crawdaddy Breaks, a labyrinth of canyons that stretched away towards the scalloped horizon.

A plume of dust in the near distance had caught his eye.

Tall and wiry for an Indian brave of the Navajo tribe, the Bear sat his horse proud and aloof, carefully studying the arid terrain floating below his vantage point. Three eagle tail-feathers tipped with white stuck out at an angle from tightly plaited black hair. Here was the sole indication, if one was needed, that this man was a natural-born leader.

The far side of the ravine was thrown into a deep shadow, in stark contrast to the brilliant splashes of red and orange daubed across the arid terrain immediately below the lip of the mesa. A narrow trail akin to a slithering asp picked its way between clumps of parched

mesquite and juniper before disappearing into a branch canyon.

High overhead, banks of high cumulus were the only blot on an otherwise unblemished ceiling of blue. But in the distance far to the west, flashes of lightning heralded the approach of what could be a desert storm. One of those occasional visitations that mother nature chose to bestow on her lethargic offspring. Onslaughts of turbulence that brought the desert to life. Only then, for the briefest of interludes, would the parched stands of yucca, prickly pear, strawberry cactus and ocotillo burst forth into full colour.

Such moments are rare instances in time, to be savoured before the relentless heat of the desert sucks the life-giving moisture from the land, once again returning it to a state of torpid indolence.

The Indian lifted a goatskin to his thin lips and drank sparingly. This was indeed a dry land, with water more valuable than the yellow rock that had driven the white invaders to steal their land. Within the hour, the storm might well arrive and briefly fill the creeks and waddies. On the other hand, the gods of the sky might just be flexing their muscles, testing the Bear's resolve. The Navajo smiled an acceptance of the challenge.

Behind him, two dozen warriors were ranged in line, awaiting their leader's signal. Their tanned faces daubed with streaks of paint told that this was no peaceful venture. Each boasted a bow slung across broad shoulders, plus a full quiver of flighted arrows. Only Stalking Bear possessed a firearm, a .74 Sharps hunting rifle stolen the day before from a settler. The unfortunate man's scalp now adorned the warrior's snakeskin belt.

For upwards of a month, the small group of renegades had been riding almost non-stop on a mission of vengeance, to fulfil a fervent pledge to their forebears for revenge on those who had betrayed them to the white eyes. Perhaps it was the blue coats who had forced his people off their homelands in Northern Arizona, but the black-hearted Utes had conspired for their own ends to imprison their neighbours. For this betrayal, they would pay the ultimate price.

And Stalking Bear was adamant their death would not be swift.

Ever since the Long March of 1864 to Bosque Redondo near Fort Sumner, the Navajo chief had sworn an oath of revenge against those responsible for the deaths of his mother and youngest sister. Hundreds more had also died through sickness and starvation on the gruelling forced trek to their new home in New Mexico. Called 'relocation' by the authorities, it was nothing short of a massacre.

Then a young brave, it was Stalking Bear's ingenuity and hunting prowess with a bow and arrow that had prevented his own early demise. And never a day had passed since when he had not prayed for retribution against the perpetrators. One white eyes especially would pay dearly – Captain Daniel Heggerty, a scout with the First Cavalry of New Mexico Volunteers. It was he who had led the soldiers directly to their camp from information supplied by the treacherous Utes.

Far worse, however, to Stalking Bear was the fact that the scout had taken his elder sister for his woman.

Over the years since that fateful decimation during the Civil War, government hand-outs of food and clothing had, in Stalking Bear's eyes, made his fellow Navajos lazy and indolent. Few wanted to face the hardship of being branded a rebel with the consequent danger such a life would surely entail.

Only in recent months had the proud Navajo been able

to persuade enough like-minded braves to abandon their sedentary lifestyle on the reservation and follow him on a trail of vengeance.

And now their quest was approaching its culmination.

'Whispering Owl!'

The summons was addressed to a round-faced stocky Indian who nudged his piebald forward beside that of his leader. Stalking Bear handed him a telescope, another trophy stolen from an inebriated soldier at Fort Sumner. The chief smiled to himself on recalling that the man had been awarded fourteen days' punishment duty for the loss which he could not explain to his commanding officer.

He pointed to a promontory some quarter-mile distant which offered a more expansive view of the surrounding terrain.

'Take the glass and tell me what you see,' ordered Stalking Bear.

'What must I look for, O Chief?' replied Whispering Owl.

'That dust devil might come from the winds that blow, or from the hoofs of those we seek. How many are they, and where are they heading?'

The Indian nodded his understanding. If any of Stalking Bear's men could spot danger it was Whispering Owl. Even the legendary bald eagle was no match for the sharp-eyed brave. The Indian dug his heels into the horse and galloped across the flat top of the mesa.

Within ten minutes, he was back blurting out his report in a staccato rush.

'Four men and a woman riding in single file along the base of the ravine.'

'White eyes?'

'Yes,' replied Whispering Owl before hurrying on, 'and the one in the lead . . .' He paused meaningfully, '. . . has

105

long black hair, face whiskers and is dressed in buckskins.'

Stalking Bear tensed, the tightness of his chiselled jaw set in stone, an implacable cast to his brown eyes. Tinged a dark mahogany, they narrowed to thin slits. Could this be the hated Trapper Dan? Was his quest nearing its end? Burnt knuckles showed white as they held the old Sharps in a vicelike grip.

The red walls of the canyon, vertical and smooth as glass, soared overhead concentrating the heat. It was hot enough to melt the eyes of a prairie dog. Heads drooping in empathy with their horses, the line of riders plodded on, following in the wake of their guide.

Mace Cavanagh removed his bandanna and stroked away the sweat dribbling down his face. God, it sure was hot and no mistake.

'What I couldn't do to a nice cold beer,' he announced to a skulking coyote.

'You can have a tubful of Champagne to bathe in once we get our hands on all that loot,' Miller said to him. 'We oughta be getting close by now.'

That was a cue for the Brazos Kid. He spurred his mount forward to draw in front of the trapper, forcing him to rein up.

'How much further, Heggerty?' he snapped. 'You ain't tryin' to pull a fast one I hope. For your sake.' His hand strayed to the butt of his revolver. 'It's been five days already and I'd hate for you to cut out and go after that treasure on your own.'

A sardonic shift of expression came over the trapper's hairy visage.

'Now how could I do that when your boss has kept a firm grip on the map.' He didn't wait for the young gunslinger to reply. 'If you want a share in this haul, that is supposin' we ain't on some kinda wild-goose chase, then I suggest you get outa my way and shut up.'

Heggerty's voice had taken on a biting edge, partly on account of the Kid's surly attitude – Brazos had that effect on most people – but mainly to hide his growing awareness that once they had found the hidden cache, his life wouldn't be worth a plugged nickel. He settled a cold glare on the Kid.

It was Miller who intervened, breaking the tension.

'So how far d'yuh reckon?'

Heggerty relaxed as the Kid snorted, then viciously dragged his mount's head round and spurred off back to the rear of the small column.

'See that clump of juniper over by the side canyon yonder?' They all followed the line of Heggerty's pointing finger. 'Well, that there's Johnson Canyon. We've arrived.'

'Don't look much to me,' grunted the Kid.

'What d'you expect? A signboard for all the world to see?' Even Cavanagh's normally placid demeanour was wearing thin where the Kid was concerned.

He would be glad to have his share of the loot and kiss these turkeys goodbye for ever. No more living on the edge just one step ahead of the law, always looking over your shoulder.

No siree. Mace Cavanagh was heading for California and the high life. Maybe buy into a hotel with flunkeys to do his bidding, or open up one of them fancy eating-houses with tablecloths and the best food. He sighed at the thought, a languid smile edging across the seamy contours of his grizzled face. His eyes, half-closed, were already savouring what he figured was going to be a very comfortable future.

His dreamy reflections were cut short by the raucous blast of a high-powered rifle echoing round the confines of the deep cutting.

*

Will Brennan would have passed the old shack by had it not been for the keen gaze of his partner.

'What's that over yonder?' enquired Ben Cassidy, drawing his dun mare to a halt.

Brennan's thoughts had been elsewhere. With the gold he hoped to dig out of his claim in Nevada, the open prairies of Canada beckoned like a flaming beacon. Wheat farming was the future. Or so he'd read. The eastern cities were crying out for bread just like they'd been willing to pay any price for beef after the Civil War had ended back in 'sixty-five.

Then he thought of the girl. Would someone like her take to the farming life? He doubted it. Too much like hard work. Them Eastern dames were like spoilt kids. All flouncy dresses and frilly underwear.

'You hear me, feller?'

The raised voice brought Will back to his current situation.

'Eh?'

'Over by that rocky overhang. Can't you see a shack?' His strident voice had taken on a hint of impatience. 'Could be those desperadoes sheltered there during the storm.'

In the fading light of late afternoon, the weathered cabin blended perfectly into its austere surroundings. It was lucky that Cassidy had been alert. Will chided himself. He was supposed to be the one in charge. This was his country. To be caught napping by some hick from back East jarred his pride somewhat.

When they caught up with Duke Miller and the gang, he would need to keep the full complement of his wits sharpened.

That was, *if* they caught up.

Will had no illusions regarding the huge task they had embarked upon. This was lonely country with few trails. And not having approached the Crawdaddy Breaks from the west before, he was largely playing it by ear. Not that he could allow Ben Cassidy ever to suspect that. Confidence and a brash disregard for danger had always seen him through before. It still would – if Lady Luck was on his side.

Will nudged his horse off the trail and led the way over to the small shack. Fifty yards short, he signalled the man following to halt behind a cluster of boulders.

He drew his revolver and thumbed back the hammer to half-cock.

'Keep me covered with that Marlin,' he said, casting an admiring glance at the fine sporting rifle. 'No sense gettin' our heads blowed off if some jasper's in occupation.'

With a stealth born from innumerable forays into general stores and emporia at dead of night in pursuit of supplies for the Blackhawks, Will sidled up to the blind side of the old shack. He paused, an ear cocked for any sign of life.

Silence hung empty on the desert wind.

Will signalled his partner forward. Inside, it was obvious that the place had only recently been vacated. Unwashed dishes lay strewn around. A stack of deer hides, pressed and strung, were ready for shipment. Wandering over to a shelf by the only window, Will picked up a faded painting of an Indian girl. She was clad in buckskins, hair neatly plaited with coloured beads; he assumed this must be the occupier's squaw.

So where was everyone?

'Appears as if this place was abandoned sudden-like,' suggested Will, poking about in cupboards.

Cassidy grunted. A second later, he gasped a terse exclamation of surprise. Will spun on his heel, right hand dropping instinctively to the holstered gun on his hip. What he perceived was his partner holding up a white square of linen decorated with lace around the edges.

'What's that?'

Cassidy's eyes misted over.

'See this?' he murmured, prodding at the corner of the handkerchief.

'What about it?' enquired a puzzled Will Brennan.

'There. At the corner embroidered in red.' A catch in his throat was quickly shrugged off. This was no time for histrionics. The twin letters 'JF' sprang from the delicate cloth. 'I had it made specially to wrap her engagement ring in.' To Cassidy, it was a shattering confirmation of his loved one's probable fate. He turned away to hide the desolation that threatened to overwhelm him.

But to Will Brennan, unimpeded by such depth of feeling, it was a clear sign that they were definitely heading in the right direction. And not far behind either. The ash in the grate was barely more than two days old.

'You know what this means?' he said, infusing a measure of passion into what was more a statement of fact than a question.

Cassidy failed to respond. Shoulders hunched, his struggle to preserve an outward air of stoic resolve had shrivelled like a desiccated apple. Will hurried on regardless. 'That gal of yours sure ain't wet behind the ears.'

The excited edge in Will's tone impinged on his partner's dulled brain. He lifted a curled eyebrow questioningly.

'What are you getting at?' he enquired cautiously.

'She left that 'kerchief as a sign for us to know she's still alive, and so's we could follow their trail.' Will handed the

110

small square of silk to his partner. 'And like as not there'll be more of the same.'

This disclosure had the effect of a three star French brandy on Cassidy. His eyes lit up, the dying embers rekindled.

'We can stay here for the night and make an early start at sun-up,' suggested Will, poking at the ash in the grate with the intention of kindling a new fire.

'How much daylight is left?' Cassidy felt suddenly reinvigorated. His dark brown eyes burned with a fresh intensity.

'Maybe two hours at the most,' said Will.

'Then let's hit the trail. Every second lost means them damn blasted sons-of-bitches are getting further away.' Cassidy moved purposefully to the open door checking the load on his .38 Lightning. 'Besides, there's no way I could stay a night in this hovel thinking on what might have happened to my beloved Jane.' For the briefest of seconds, the newly kindled fire appeared to wane. Then he turned back to Brennan.

'You coming or staying?'

There was no hint of compromise in the query. Will cocked a quizzical peeper at his associate. That was the first time he had heard the guy utter anything like an expletive. He sighed, threw down the stick he had been poking in the grate, and stood up. Two hours wouldn't make a fig of difference to their pursuit of the gang. But if it kept the dude alert, on guard and ready for the inevitable clash, then who was he to discourage such fervour.

'Give me ten minutes to see if there's anything we can use. Then I'll be with you.' Will handed over a bag of oats. 'Make sure the animals are well fed before we leave. It's unlikely we'll meet up with anyone else from here on. And

111

there are no relay stations where we're headin'.'

Cassidy nodded.

It was a good twenty minutes before Will eventually emerged from inside the shack, his arms loaded down with all manner of goodies.

'This feller sure didn't believe in skimpin' hisself.' Will smiled.

'I see you're rather partial to the taste of tinned peaches,' replied his partner, casting an amused smirk at the gaudy labels on the cans. 'Not to mention . . .' Screwing up his eyes, he slowly read the legend on the other cans '. . . Irish stew! What in thunderation is that?'

'Never tasted it,' answered Will, grinning widely, 'but there's always a first time for everything.' Quickly he stashed away the fresh supplies on the back of the pack-mule.

By the time the odd duo were once again heading east, their supplies greatly enhanced at the expense of their unknown benefactor, the rosy hue of late afternoon had been tempered to a soft lilac.

NINE

MEXICAN STAND-OFF

Mace Cavanagh never knew what hit him. One minute he was dreamily ruminating on a bright future, the next thing his life was snuffed out by a lethal chunk of lead burying itself in his skull. Like a discarded rag-doll, the war veteran was flung from his horse as the harsh clamour of the rifle shot echoed around the confines of the canyon. Pink globules of brain matter splattered the rider immediately behind.

The Brazos Kid emitted a choking yell of panic. Whilst desperately clawing at the glutinous mess splayed across his hawkish features, he threw himself from the saddle and scuttled behind a tumble of rocks at the side of the trail.

Another shot rang out, removing Duke Miller's Stetson but thankfully leaving his head in one piece.

Ever the paternalistic leader, he was still able to issue instructions, even if they were a mite obvious and rather unnecessary under the circumstances.

'Take cover! And keep your heads down!'

113

His raucous bellow was drowned by a full-throated series of cries from the top end of the canyon. A dozen redskins, smeared with paint and clearly intent on adding scalps to their lodge poles, charged straight at Miller and his band. Drawing his pistol, Miller snapped off a couple of quick shots before diving for cover.

'Yeehaaar! Got one of the red bastards!'

High-octane adrenaline mixed with fear and a dash of excitement poured from his mouth as one of the renegades threw up his arms and bit the dust.

Just to his left, an arrow buried itself in the scarred trunk of a dried up juniper no more than six inches from Jane Fanshaw's head. A fearful cry of anguish was cut short by another arrow bouncing off a nearby rock. Hugging the sandy earth, Jane prayed that one set of captors was not about to be replaced by those of a far more lethal variety. At least with Miller and his gang she stood a chance of keeping her hair. But with these red savages whooping and baying for blood, the future looked decidedly bleak.

A rifle shot blasted a chunk of rock from the boulder behind which she was hiding. Fragments whistled past her ear. A sudden nip on her right cheek elicited a pained yelp. Her hand came away red with her own blood.

Brazos couldn't help chortling at the stunned expression on the girl's ashen face.

'Better say yer prayers, girlie.' He smirked. 'That sure looks like a bad wound from where I'm sittin'.'

Heggerty immediately piped up from his place of concealment on the other side of the girl.

'Don't listen to that jackass, miss. It's only a scratch.' He speared the Kid with a hard look which was received with a churlish shrug of indifference, then leaned over and patted the girl on the arm, a reassuring gesture that elicited a grateful nod of thanks.

'Here they come again.'

Miller's brittle shout was a sharp reminder of their desperate predicament. Three white men against a band of bloodthirsty Indians were not good odds. And how many others might there be in reserve? He hadn't time to ponder on the conjecture.

Pounding hoofs of unshod ponies hammered at the ground. This time they gave full vent to their terrifying throaty howl of vengeance. The smile on the Kid's face froze to a horrified rictus as he aimed his revolver. The shot missed its target. Little wonder with his hand shaking so badly.

As the first group of Indians whipped past, one flung something over the Kid's head. It looked like a couple of hanks of rope. Brazos turned, his lowering brow screwed up in puzzlement. Then he realized.

A hissing and a writhing told their own story. Loose tail-bones rattled a staccato warning. Their flat heads swaying ominously, ready to strike, the three deadly sidewinders held him in a mesmeric embrace.

For no more than a second he just stared, mouth hung open, eyes agog.

Then all hell broke loose, as the Kid dug his boot heels into the soft sand and scuttled crablike out of range of the lethal poison-packers. But now he was out into the open, exposed, with the second group of Indians bearing down with a single aim in mind. Brazos scrambled to his feet and raised his pistol.

Too late, he saw the sharpened point of the war lance thrusting at his chest. Fluttering turkey-feathers attached to the wooden shaft seemed to stun the outlaw into submission. And the rider was going fast, an ugly snarl of triumph on his daubed visage. Hugging the neck of his mount, the lethal weapon clutched firmly into his side, the

Indian known as Whispering Owl bore down rapidly on the Kid. Rooted to the spot with fear, Brazos stood no chance.

And so it was. In the blink of an eye, his lean frame was impaled on the wicked barbs and lifted clear off the dry ground. From the fatal wound, a fountain of bright scarlet arced across the canyon, staining the desert floor. Only a choking hiss gushed from the punctured torso as it was carried off down the trail.

With a snort of derision, Whispering Owl threw the lance and its grizzly appendage aside. Bulging eyes no longer of this earth stared skywards from the fallen corpse.

But the chilling acclamation of victory was to be short lived.

Heggerty quickly swivelled round and drew a bead on the disappearing back of Whispering Owl. Taking careful aim, he gently hauled back on the hair trigger of his trusted Kentucky long rifle. The black powder fired, slamming the stock into his shoulder whilst propelling the lead ball towards its fast disappearing target.

Now a hundred yards down the trail, the trapper smiled as a dark stain erupted from the Indian's bare back. A deathly wail replaced the exuberant yipping as the red man's life force evaporated and he slid from the pony's back in a jumbled heap of torn flesh.

At the same time, Miller had managed to down another.

His eyes met those of the trapper. A brief nod passed between the two. They had survived thus far, but each knew the advantage was with the Indians. The defenders' horses had stampeded at the first charge, along with all their spare ammunition.

But, most important of all, with the canteens of water.

His second-in-command now gone to meet his ancestors, Stalking Bear retired to the cover of a clump of desiccated cottonwoods with the remainder of his men to regroup. Although he could console himself with having done for two white eyes, the loss of three of his own brave warriors rankled.

Having passed close to the long-haired one, the Bear had no doubt that this was the man he sought. The man they called Trapper Dan. The man who had stolen his sister, and had then allowed her to die from the white man's disease.

Stalking Bear scowled at the thought.

But he knew he held the whip hand. Without water and trapped in the open, the white eyes would stand no chance of escaping. During the remaining hours of daylight, he and his men could avoid the unremitting heat beneath the welcome shade afforded by the cottonwoods.

Stalking Bear lifted the goatskin to his lips and drank deeply. He could afford to wait until nightfall, then sneak up and take them out one by one.

What the Indian chief did not know was that Heggerty had discovered a small spring. In reality, it was barely more than a dribble issuing from the back wall of the canyon. Nevertheless it was sufficient to sustain life. And that was what mattered.

It had been the steady drip, drip on to the hard pan behind his position that had attracted his attention. Such occurrences were rare in the canyonlands. Heggerty offered a silent prayer to his Maker.

He peered over at the girl. The blood had dried on her cheek, but she appeared exhausted: an Easterner unused to the tough ways of the frontier. He and a hardcase like Miller could probably have survived a couple of days without water – three at a pinch. But the girl? He shook his head.

Heggerty reached inside his buckskin jacket and withdrew a metal tin. Levering off the airtight lid, he emptied the contents into his hand, riffling the brown strands.

'What's that?' enquired Miller.

'The finest tobacco Virginia can produce.' Heggerty sucked air in through tightly clenched teeth. 'It'll soon dry out and turn to dust in this heat.' It was a wrench, but one that had to be made. He pushed the tin beneath the trickle.

Then he looked at Miller. 'Enough for one big smoke each. What d'yuh say?'

'Don't mind if I do,' replied the outlaw boss, accepting the thick stogie. He fired up sucking the welcome smoke down into his lungs. It was the best he had ever tasted. Maybe even his last.

Then it struck him. Outlaw Boss! What a joke. He was the only one left, and for how long? A bitter snarl split the coarsened features. Barely more than a stone's throw from a fortune in gold and it might as well have been stuck on the moon. Miller sank down beneath the rock and cogitated on what might have been. His black eyebrows met in a dark frown.

It was another hour before anyone spoke.

'When d'yuh figure them savages'll come at us again?' asked Miller, peering up the trail towards the sconse of cottonwoods. He couldn't pick out any signs of the concealed Indians. But they were there all right, no doubting that. And right beneath where the cave was located.

'They're in no hurry,' replied Heggerty. He removed the stiff-brimmed deerskin hat and wiped a day's accumulation of dirt and sweat from his face and neck. 'They'll reckon on us bein' without water. At least that gives us some advantage.' He eyed the steady drip of the life-giving elixir dribbling into the tin. 'But without horses, we ain't goin' nowhere fast.'

Her eyes closed, Jane appeared to have fallen asleep. But her breathing was unsteady, on the ragged side, smooth cheeks blotchy and red. The shallow tin was now half-full. He reached down, lifted it and tipped the contents to her mouth. The girl's dark eyes flickered open as the tepid liquid bathed her sore lips.

'Thank you,' she croaked. All too soon the tin was empty.

A brown lizard scurried across the sandy waste beside her boot. It stopped, tongue flicking the air, sensing a presence close by. Heggerty eyed it with professional interest. Good hard skin for toe caps, but too small yet awhile. His boot nudged at the static creature. Quick as flash, it disappeared into a crack between the rocks.

The trapper smiled. No such easy way out for them.

They settled down for a long wait. What was known as a Mexican stand-off.

By late afternoon Jane was becoming delirious, her mind wandering. Frequently, she would blurt out incomprehensible mutterings. The name Cassidy was mentioned along with somebody called Brennan.

Heggerty was worried. She obviously couldn't take much more. Out here in the open they were at the mercy of the desert sun beating down from a cloudless sky. The steady if slow supply of water from the spring had now shrunk to almost nothing.

'We have to do something,' he said.

With an effort, Miller raised the tip of his hat.

'What d'you suggest?' he muttered with more than a hint of sarcasm. 'We grow wings and fly?'

Heggerty ignored the jibe.

'Soon as it's dark, we sneak out,' he said. 'If we back trail, like as not we'll pick up the horses. They can't have gone far.'

119

A glint had been rekindled in Miller's grey visage once he had assimilated the distinct possibility that they might well escape from their predicament.

'What about the girl?' he asked.

'What about her?'

'She's just a liability. She'll only slow us up. I say we leave her to the tender mercy of them savages.'

'You sure are one caring guy, ain't yuh, Miller?'

'I just figure she ain't gonna make it anyhow. So why put our own lives in danger.'

Heggerty held the outlaw with a flinty gaze before replying.

'The girl comes with us.'

His tone was measured and brooked no argument. It was backed up by the long barrel of the Hawken pointing unwaveringly at Miller's face.

The outlaw shrugged. 'If you want her along, then you can do the carryin'.'

TEN

NAVAHO CUNNING

Stalking Bear had reached the same conclusion as his old enemy. The white eyes could also benefit from the onset of night. And he did not want to split his force to guard each end of the canyon.

There was, however, another way.

The cluster of boulders behind which the three white eyes were concealed lay directly at the foot of the rock wall on the north side of the canyon. All it needed was for four of his men to circle round and climb to the upper rim overlooking their quarry, create a small avalanche that would drive them out into the open.

After relaying his plan to the chosen quartet, the warriors faded into the arid landscape.

A half-hour passed.

The Navaho chief screwed up his eyes against the harsh glare and surveyed the rim. The briefest of acknowledgements and he knew that Elk Horn was in place. A dour smile playing across the weathered contours of his face betrayed no trace of humour. Only a grim determination for final retribution.

And now that time had arrived.

Turning to his men, Stalking Bear ceremoniously drew back the curled hammer lock of the Sharps and checked the cartridge loading. With the rifle clutched tightly to his chest, the renegade chief issued his final orders.

'When the rock slide is launched from the rim, we attack. If the whites are not crushed under the fall, we take them captive.' His fearsome countenance swept over the assembled warriors. 'If any tries to resist, cut him down like the wheat in the field. But leave the tall long-hair alone. He is mine.'

Overhead a mountain owl hooted. A flight of hungry buzzards floated by on the rising thermals. Circling above the killing ground, they awaited their chance to participate in the bloodletting.

Lifting his right arm, Stalking Bear gave the signal. A flurry of activity on the top of the soaring red buttress told him that the fun was about to begin. A thin trickle of dust was followed by a low growl as chunks of rock were levered into motion. Gathering pace, the boulders unhinged others in their headlong surge to the rim of the canyon wall. The chaotic mêlée, once unleashed, was now beyond recall.

Stalking Bear emitted a blood-curdling Navajo battle cry, then leathered his pony.

Like a red river, the rock splurge poured over the lip of the mesa.

It was the swirling cloud of red dust that prompted Heggerty to look skywards. His mouth gaped wide. For a split second he froze. Then a piercing screech erupted from deep within his being.

'Avalanche!'

He instantly grabbed hold of the girl and threw her to one side, prostrating himself on top of her.

122

Miller's panicking yell of terror was drowned by the thunderous din hurtling towards the ground. Scrambling away from the lethal flood of rocks into the open, he was cut down by an equally lethal hunk of lead ploughing into his head and removing half the skull in the process. As he spun round with the sudden impact, his demise was ensured by three arrows burying themselves in his chest.

Stalking Bear wrenched his mount viciously to a juddering halt and leapt from its blanketed back.

Where was long-hair? Was he dead, crushed beneath the weight of rock? Or was he even now aiming to make a fight of it?

The Indian crouched behind his fallen mount, removed the spent cartridge and thumbed in a fresh round. He patted the weapon appreciatively. No wonder the blue coats had defeated most of the western tribes, forcing them on to the hated reservations. With more guns like this, he Stalking Bear could once again command respect from the whites, and achieve honour for his tribe.

He edged forward warily, trying to pierce the choking haze that now filled the base of the enclosed ravine. Glancing idly at his chattering warriors, a disdainful cast smothered the leathery features. He scoffed derisively. They were as children. Too busy squabbling over the hair of the dead outlaw to recall that the other white man could at this very moment be waiting to shoot them down.

Slowly the dust settled. Still no movement from among the mass of fallen rocks.

He called to his men as Elk Horn raised Miller's dripping scalp aloft.

'Now you have all had your fun, remember our task is still not complete.'

Hurriedly the renegades notched fresh arrows into

their bowstrings, their painted faces assuming a suitably ferocious expression.

'Spread out and search for the other two white eyes,' ordered Stalking Bear sharply, whilst remaining behind his horse.

It was a brave called Grey Cloud who made the discovery his chief had been awaiting. Youngest of the band, Cloud was something of a hothead, but eager to please and always in the thickest of any skirmishes they had engaged in.

'Over here, Bear,' he called excitedly, waving his hand.

A look of satisfaction twisted Stalking Bear's tense expression as he swaggered casually across the stony floor of the canyon.

Slowly the opaque layers of darkness began to lift from Dan Heggerty's brutalized mind. Replaced by a turgid grey, consciousness returned him to the harsh reality of his situation. Twisting his head to avoid the sun's remorseless fury, he discovered that tough rawhide thongs securely pinioned both hands and feet to the desert floor.

With full consciousness came the pain.

'Aaaaagh!' he groaned. A wave of throbbing agony rippled through his taut frame. But at least he was still alive. And where there was life . . . But for how long? And what had happened to the girl? Screwing up his eyes against the ferocious glare, he could see that Miller was dead.

He tried to move. But any movement other than a turn of the head was impossible.

All he could remember was throwing himself over the girl.

Then – nothing.

'So, white eyes. You have seen fit to answer my prayer to the Great One.'

Peering up at the shadow that now thankfully obscured the sun, Heggerty picked out other dark forms surrounding him.

'You have been asleep for over a moon,' continued the stentorian voice. 'I was beginning to think you would never return to this world. And that would have been sad, a great shame.'

'Ugh?' grunted the captive.

'You will not recognize me, white man. But I know you.' A cruel nuance had crept into the Indian's stilted drone. A twisted smile hazed the warped features. It was not a pleasant sight.

Not a man easily disturbed, at that moment Heggerty smelt fear.

Stalking Bear sensed the other man's disquiet. He uttered a repulsive snort of throaty laughter. The other braves joined him.

'Captain Daniel Heggerty – scout for the New Mexico Volunteers.' All semblance of hilarity had evaporated on the desert wind as Stalking Bear lashed out with his rawhide quirt at the supine captive. A bright red weal instantly formed across Heggerty's right cheek, globules of blood oozing from the savage blow. 'The one who led the blue coats directly to our camp in the Chuska Mountains.'

The Navaho chief was now screaming obscenities at his prisoner.

'And then you paid my family the worst insult possible by carrying off my sister to your bed. For that you will die. By the time I have finished, *Trapper Dan*,' Heggerty's nickname was spat back into his bloodied face, 'you will beg me, plead with me to draw your miserable life to a speedy close.'

Mention of his deceased wife brought recognition. Haunted eyes locked on to those of his tormentor.

'Stalking Bear!'

'Yes, Heggerty. It is I, Stalking Bear, who now has you at my mercy.'

'But I loved your sister with all my being,' rasped Heggerty, desperately trying to evoke some measure of compassion in his bitter opponent, this man who was his brother-in-law. 'She was my life. It was the fever that killed her.'

'The white man's fever,' snarled Stalking Bear.

'I did everything possible to save her.'

'It was not enough. She died.' The Indian's eyes were dead, his look cold and merciless. 'And now so must you.'

'What about the girl who was with me?' enquired Heggerty. 'What have you done with her?'

'You took my sister for your own. Now I will have this girl. She will make a good addition to my tepee.' Even with the midday sun broiling his innards, Heggerty shivered beneath the withering smile of his captor. The implications for Jane were all too obvious. He vented his anger and frustration with a wholesale utterance of expletives.

'You lowdown mangy cur! What sort of worthless bastard are you?'

But it was all to no avail. His futile struggles to release the tight rawhide bonds met with another round of derisive laughter.

'Rant all you wish, white man. The girl is mine. To do with as I so choose.' Stalking Bear's lurid visage blazed with a fervid lust. 'Yes indeed.' He smirked, leering at his companions. 'Her body is that from which dreams are made, her skin smooth as the night breeze. I will give her the honour of keeping me warm when snow blankets the land.'

126

The evil grin slid from his swarthy features.

'But enough of this prattle,' he chided, resuming a more rigid tone. 'You, Heggerty, are not the only reason for my return to the canyonlands. Those treacherous Ute parasites who betrayed my people have their main encampment no more than a day's ride to the north. Once I have burned them out and shown the dogs that one Navaho warrior is worth a hundred Ute vermin, I will return here.'

He turned to his new subordinate. The wily brave standing resolutely to his left had willingly taken the place of the deceased Whispering Owl. He had often likened the hawk-eyed one to an old squaw. Sly and devious, Running Fox was well named.

'Bring my horse.' Stalking Bear infused an imperious tone into the terse command.

A brief pause followed. With a curl of the lip he added, 'Also the girl, so this low-life can see she is unharmed. Then he will truly understand the pleasurable future that awaits her. At the same time, the snake in the grass can think well on his own fate.'

Then to the eager Grey Cloud he nodded towards a mound close to the tethered prisoner. The youth glanced at the two foot high pyramid and immediately caught on to his chief's thinking.

He smirked knowingly.

'Stalking Bear has supped with the Wise One Above to think of such a torment,' he rejoiced, poking the heap with his war lance.

All eyes were fixed on the knobbly mound, including those of an apprehensive Trapper Dan. For a few seconds nothing happened. Then the first ants appeared. Large soldier ants at least a half-inch in length, scurrying hither and thither, angry at being disturbed in their lair.

Stalking Bear ambled over to his captive and casually prodded his bare shoulder with a lance tip. Heggerty winced as the steel bit into his exposed flesh but remained silent. He had no intention of surrendering his dignity to these savages, even if he had to surrender his life. A trickle of blood issued from the tiny wound.

With the steel tip dripping crimson, the warrior chief dabbed a thin trail across to the anthill.

'The life force of man is irresistible to all creatures of the earth,' he said. 'Even a lowly ant.'

Then he mounted up, swinging the pony's head to the north facing canyon. His men followed suit.

'Let us trust, white man, that these creatures leave some part of your miserable hide for me to play with upon my return. If not . . .'

He shrugged carelessly and grabbed hold of the tie rein attached to Jane Fanshaw's horse. The animal gave a brief whinny then trotted off behind the lead horse.

'Tonight we celebrate our good fortune, my braves. And I promise you that before the sun sets on one more day, the Ute dogs will have joined the spirits of their ancestors to wander for ever in the swamplands of eternal damnation.'

The Indian uttered a throaty yarrop. He was enjoying himself. The other renegades milled around whooping and cheering with passionate anticipation.

To Jane Fanshaw, it felt as though she was entombed in a living nightmare. Lost in a darkened maze with no way out. But this was no fantasy world. Tomorrow she would awake to find her nightmare was only too real.

The idea of this brutal savage laying a finger on her was beyond conjecture. She would rather die first.

As her horse trotted passed, the girl peered down at the blood-caked body of Trapper Dan Heggerty. Even though he had aided and abetted her kidnappers, the man had saved her life when he had pushed her beneath the rocky overhang at the base of the cliff. For that she should have been grateful. He had sustained severe injuries to the head and back from falling debris, all to save her.

But wouldn't instant death from the rock fall have been preferable for both of them to what was their unenviable lot.

Now it was too late.

Their eyes met briefly. She sensed the man's strength, his resilience, willing her to be strong also. A brief nod to indicate that she understood, then the moment had passed. But would she have the tenacity, the innate resources to maintain her sanity in the face of such abasement?

Jane doubted it. No. There was only one way out.

She offered up a silent prayer of forgiveness for what had to be done.

Stalking Bear emitted a yell of animalistic fervour. He smote the fetid air with a flourish, then led his small yet defiant group along the side ravine known as Johnson Canyon.

Had he known that little more than a few hundred yards away a vast treasure was purported to be concealed, the renegade leader would have shown no interest. Those trifles that the white eyes held in high esteem were far removed from the things valued by the red man. And at this moment, Stalking Bear yearned for revenge against his sworn enemies. Anything else was of secondary importance.

A flight of buzzards anxious to partake in the rare treat spread out below them cawed in feverish anticipation. Squawks of alarm were aimed at the scurrying line of ants. But they went unheeded. And as long as the securely bound delicacy could still draw breath, the feathered predators would keep their distance. Buzzards only feasted on carrion.

Bleakly eyeing the black-winged predators circling in the azure void above, Heggerty struggled and writhed to discourage any temptation they might have to check on his condition.

At the same time, his tight gaze focused on the advancing line of ants. Slow and measured, their progress towards him was unwavering.

Will Brennan and Ben Cassidy had made good progress since leaving the trapper's shack. The threatened storm had thankfully veered away to the north. Distant crackles of lightning lit up the darkening sky to their left – the ensuing rumbles of thunder more faint as time passed.

That was when they heard the gunfire. The deep boom of a rifle followed by snapping yelps characteristic of a handgun.

Putting spurs to their animal's flanks, the two riders tore along the dried-up arroyo trying to ascertain the source of the dissonant clamour. But the uneven terrain of the Crawdaddy Breaks made it difficult to locate.

'Which way d'you reckon?' yelled Cassidy above the pounding of the hoofs.

'Hard to say,' replied Will, sensing that the noise was becoming more faint. He signalled his partner to slow down to a gentle trot. 'These side canyons play strange tricks on the mind.'

'Makes for a knotty problem, then.' Cassidy added as an afterthought.

'Sure does.'

'What we gonna do then?'

That was when another raucous bellow assailed their ears.

It was like thunder but rougher, more of a menacing growl. And much closer than any previous outburst.

As one, they both turned towards a tumble of boulders on their left atop a brush-cloaked knoll.

'Over there!' snapped Will.

Cassidy nodded with vigour.

The slope was too steep for their horses to negotiate. They hitched them to a nearby yucca stem, then scrambled up the steeply canting incline. High-heeled riding-boots made for an arduous climb with loose gravel impeding their progress. Choking dust turned their parched throats to sandpaper.

It took a full hour to reach the upper limit of the loose knot of rocks. Beyond lay a half-mile of rough plateau deeply scored by hidden gullies. The anxious pair were forced to curtail their headlong dash when Cassidy tumbled into one of the narrow fissures, twisting his leg in the process.

Luckily, nothing was broken. But a three inch gash across his calf muscle had to be attended to. After slitting the right leg of Cassidy's store-bought trousers, Will stanched the crimson flow and bandaged the wound tightly using his necker. Thereafter, progress slowed to a snail's pace.

At long last, however, they crested the last rise.

A scene from the devil's playground met their angst-ridden gaze.

Bodies littered the confines of the ravine, their limbs contorted at ungainly angles. Dark patches of dried blood had stained the sandy waste. Already, feathered predators were gorging on the still warm flesh, black bills dripping red.

'Are we too late?' croaked Cassidy, his wavering voice no more than a hoarse whisper. He was eyeing the awful scene, desperately searching for signs of his loved one. 'Can you see her?'

But Brennan hadn't heard. Already he was clattering down the loose shale, waving his hat and frantically hallooing to frighten off the gore-caked scavengers. Squawking loudly with more that a hint of frustration at having been so unceremoniously disturbed, the buzzards nonetheless dispersed. Large wings flapping angrily, they retired to a safe haven atop a clump of cottonwoods to observe proceedings. Cowards at heart, they had no stomach for confronting living creatures the size of humans.

Hobbling behind, face contorted with pain from the pummelling his injured leg was having to endure, Cassidy reached ground level at last. Once there, he ranged across the canyon floor delving into every hidden crevice in search of his fiancée.

'Jane! Jane!'

His desperate calls went unanswered.

From high on the crest of the rocky knoll, Will's eagle eye had picked out the splayed body of a white man stretched out some way beyond the immediate site of battle. Approaching the staked-out captive, he thought for a moment that the man was dead. Then a low groan issued from blistered lips.

But what caused Brennan most alarm were the hoards of scurrying insects literally eating the man alive. He was covered in ants.

'Over here quick!' he yelled back at his partner. The harsh timbre stayed Cassidy's frenetic rummaging among the jumbled chaos of smashed boulders. He looked towards Brennan. 'There's a man still alive over here. But only just.'

Cassidy hurried across the open ground. What he saw has a half-naked man tethered by his hands and feet face up.

'Good God!'

The man's shredded body was a mass of tiny lacerations. Its similarity to a piece of meat on a butcher's slab did not go unnoticed. Cassidy stood there, mouth agape.

'Don't just stand there,' railed Brennan who was feverishly trying to brush the heaving mass from the poor guy's body. 'Cut him free so's we can drag him away from this ant hill. It's the blood that attracts them.'

Cassidy slashed at the hide thongs with his Bowie knife. Quickly, they hauled the bleeding hunk of flesh over to a piece of shade beneath a cottonwood. Will hurried over to a grazing horse and unhooked the water bottle. He bathed the man's blotched face with water, dribbling small amounts between the swollen lips. The man expectorated with a grating cough as the life-giving moisture took effect.

It took a further twenty minutes before the last ant was dispatched. Another fifteen before the man was able to open his eyes. Bloodshot and watery, they looked at Will with a dull flatness.

Will held his partner with a fervent gaze. And shook his head.

The guy was close to death.

But before he went to meet his Maker, it was imperative they learn what had happened – and if Jane Fanshaw had survived. Will levered the man into a sitting position, his back propped against the tree trunk.

Eventually he spoke. The words were slow and faltering.

'We were ambushed . . . taken by surprise . . . bunch o' renegade Navajos.' The man grabbed Will by the arm, his grip surprisingly firm. Wild staring eyes bulged now like organ stops. 'Nothin' I could do . . . nothin' I could do.' Then he sank back totally exhausted.

'Take it easy, mister,' advised Will with a cool detachment he certainly didn't feel. 'Just give us the gist of what happened in your own time.'

Slowly, the gruesome events leading up to the slaughter began to unfold. Both rescuers fought down their impatience when the dying man fell silent. Each time he resurfaced, the trembling voice was that much weaker, his utterances less coherent.

It was the uncontrollable shuddering, the chattering teeth, that told them the end was near. The clammy skin took on a bluish hue. Eyes that were half-closed flickered once, then slowly rolled up as the grim reaper, the harbinger of death, finally came a-calling.

Will Brennan sighed deeply. A shiver ran through his whole being. A single teardrop carved out a trail down his stubbled face. With exaggerated deference, he carefully lowered the man to the ground, drawing his eyelids down. Trapper Dan Heggerty had been a living legend to all those who sought out adventure on the south-west frontier of the United States. He would be sorely missed.

It was Cassidy who broke in on his ruminations.

'Hadn't we oughta be trailing out after this crazy bunch of Navajo savages,' he pressed, rising to his feet.

Will remained still, silent, kneeling beside the deceased trapper.

Cassidy nudged him with his boot. 'They can't be more than three hours ahead.'

'Give me a minute.'

'But every second wasted places Jane in greater danger,' urged Cassidy his voice rising appreciably.

'Listen to me, greenhorn, you heard what I said,' rasped Will, his voice barely above a cold hiss. 'If'n you want somethin' to do, ride back down the trail and collect our mounts. I need time to figure out what's best to do from here on.'

The rebuke stung Cassidy. His hackles rose. Benjamin

Cassidy was not used to being spoken to in such a brusque manner. With a considerable effort, he held himself in check, recognizing when it was best to keep his peace. Without another word, he gathered up one of the loose horses and swung into the saddle, digging his spurred boots into the animal's flanks. A hundred yards down the trail he hauled rein and looked back. Brennan was still kneeling down beside the dead man.

His head appeared to be bowed, hands clasped together as if in prayer.

What Cassidy did not know was that Daniel Heggerty was, or had been, Will's long-lost uncle. His mother's elder brother, Dan had left home at an early age due to some family dispute with their father. Will never did learn the truth of the matter. And now he never would. It must have been a serious disagreement. For the man never again returned to the family home back in Kentucky.

By means of newspaper reports and the frontier grapevine, Will had avidly followed Trapper Dan's exploits. At some stage in his life he had hoped to eventually meet this celebrated relative and backwoodsman. Never in his wildest dreams could Will Brennan have foreseen how such a meeting would finally occur.

When Cassidy returned a half-hour later, Will was his normal placid self. The Easterner's face creased into a puzzled frown as he noted the other man's somewhat lazy smile. Why had Brennan suddenly adopted this smug manner?

Brennan accepted the reins of his horse and mounted up. After checking the load on his Winchester, he pointed a gloved finger at the line of unshod hoof marks heading into the side canyon.

'That's the way they went,' he opined. 'I reckon from what Heggerty told me, they'll rest up overnight before hitting the Ute camp around dawn tomorrow. Chances are they'll take your fiancée with them. If we aim to save her hide, it'll mean us sneakin' up on 'em after dark. Then makin' a dash for it.'

He laid a steady look on his comrade, casting a jaundiced eye down to the crimson bandage wrapped around Cassidy's leg.

'Could be we'll hit trouble. You up for that, mister?' he asked, rolling a quirley and offering it to the other man. Cassidy accepted the placatory gesture with a nod of thanks, then fired up. He coughed drily as the powerful bite stung his throat. As a rule he never touched anything other than the finest Havana cigars. But this was no time for displays of aloof superiority.

In silence and holding Brennan's cool gaze, he casually lifted the Marlin from its leather boot and checked the loading. Brennan smiled, admiring the tenderfoot's raw determination. He must clearly love the girl. A twinge of envy plucked at Will's heart-strings. But only for an instant.

'They won't be expectin' company. With a bitta luck, we can be in and out with no shots being fired.'

'Let's hope so,' muttered Cassidy, replacing the rifle.

As the pair made to follow the Indian trail into Johnson Canyon, Cassidy noticed a pile of stones to one side under the shade of a lone piñon, a small wooden cross at its head. Brennan offered the lonely grave a brief salute as he passed.

'He must have been one hell of a guy,' Cassidy observed ruefully.

'You could say that,' responded Will, wrenching his head away from the grave towards the ramparts hemming them in on either side.

ELEVEN

INDIAN CAMP

It was well after dark when a pale glow diffused the stygian gloom ahead of them. A heavy silence, pregnant with brooding menace, hung in the oppressive atmosphere. Both men recognized the signs. This was the point of no return.

'We'll leave the horses here,' whispered Will, peering through the gloom towards the small encampment in a clearing. 'Leave your rifle here,' he said to his partner. 'A handgun can do much more damage in these confined spaces.'

Guns drawn, they advanced along the bottom of the canyon, carefully picking their way between the loose jumble of rocks. Even though the distance was no more than 200 yards, progress was slow. It was imperative to avoid making any noise that might arouse the camp residents.

Shadowy images looming out of the darkness set their taut nerves on edge. Twisted junipers, ragged and still, prickly pear bunching together, innocent rock clusters dark and forbidding. Each one could have been an Indian standing guard. And each had to be silently investigated.

As it turned out, the renegades must have considered themselves to be invincible, safe from attack. Who else could possibly know they were in this remote canyon?

The camp was deathly silent.

Only the fire emitted a faint crackling, a haunting refrain floating on the light breeze. In the dim light, rounded shapes lay huddled beneath their colourfully woven blankets. The Indian ponies were picketed on the far side of the clearing.

Will peered down at his watch. It read twenty after four. It would soon be dawn. They didn't have much time.

But where was Jane?

Reluctantly, Will came the conclusion that they would have to separate, each circling the encampment from opposite sides to locate the missing captive. And they could only pray that she was still alive.

Cassidy nodded his understanding of his partner's gesticulations, then slid off to the right. Will edged carefully to the left.

An owl hooted in the distance, searching for its next meal. Will envied the creature its capacity to see in the dark. He could only feel his way with the utmost care, gingerly probing the darkness just beyond the glow cast by the camp-fire.

Half-way round the camp, his hand brushed against what could only be a buckskin-clad leg. It shifted momentarily, then settled down. He froze. Beads of sweat broke out on his forehead. A chill raced down his spine.

Then he saw her, leaning against a rock, her head sunk low, hands and feet securely tied. Ragged breathing informed him that this was the sleep of a highly troubled mind. For a full minute he remained still, unmoving, hardly daring to breathe himself.

At the far side of the clearing, a brief yet harsh scrape of leather on stone indicated the position of his partner. It sounded like a herd of rampaging elephants to Will's acute ear. A horse snickered, sensing an alien presence.

Gently, almost reluctantly, he shook the girl's leg. A choking gurgle escaped from her mouth. Will knew she was about to cry out in shocked panic. Quickly he clamped a hand firmly over the open orifice. A muted 'hush' to quieten her anxiety, then he murmured calmly yet with a firm conviction:

'This is Will Brennan. Are you OK? They haven't hurt you, have they?'

He waited tensely until her nod assured him that she was uninjured and had control of her faculties. Then released his hand from her mouth.

'No time to explain now but I have your fiancé with me. We've come to get you out of here.'

'Ben, here?' she queried.

Will gestured with his thumb. 'Over the far side of the camp.'

His briskly confident manner allayed the girl's fears. It was, however, a self-assurance that Will was only able to maintain due to the darkness. Had she witnessed the anxious frown of doubt that haunted his pinched features, Jane's hopes of escaping alive from her night-mare would have instantly dissolved in the chilling air. Will prayed fervently that his nickname would justify itself and provide for their salvation. Certainly luck would play a major role in a successful escape from Johnson Canyon.

He slit through the rough strips of leather that bound her hands and feet carefully helping Jane Fanshaw to her feet. Gritting her teeth, she stifled groans of pain as cramp attacked constricted muscles. Yet even in her dazed stupor, Jane realized that silence was of paramount importance. Any commotion, and their plans would be thrown into disarray.

That was when it happened.

Ben Cassidy had stumbled and fallen. His pistol chinked against a rock close to the group of tethered horses. Disturbed by this unfamiliar intrusion, one skittish mare emitted a frightened whinny. This was followed immediately by another. And like a tumbling pack of cards, the whole remuda was soon panicking and tugging at their hitching lines.

The cat was well and truly out of the bag now. So much for Will Brennan's lucky streak.

Although it was a fallacy that Indians always slept with one eye open, renegades were by nature light sleepers. The disturbance immediately found half a dozen throwing off their blankets. Will didn't wait for them to retaliate. Grabbing at the revolver on his hip, he pumped a couple of shots into the lurid shadows reflected in the light of the camp-fire. Flame lanced from the bucking six shooter. He had the satisfaction of seeing one Indian scream and throw up his arms as the lethal hunks of lead smashed into his body. One less to worry about. Totally unexpected, the ambush threw the Indians into disarray.

Will took full advantage of the milling disorder.

'Cut the picket line!' he shouted trusting that Cassidy would have the acumen to capitalize on their situation. 'Scatter the horses!'

The Easterner had not become president of a major cattle company through inheritance alone.

'Sure thing,' came back the confident reply. He slit the line and waved his hat at the bunched ponies.

Already the eastern sky was showing signs of approaching day. A grey sheen rose slowly above the ragged peaks like some giant curtain. Changing gradually to a dull ochre, it would be another hour before the blazing orb eventually made its appearance.

To promote further confusion, Will removed a stick from inside his shirt and aimed it towards the spluttering remnants of the fire.

'Keep your head down, Ben,' he yelled loosing off another couple of shells. Grasping the girl's hand, he pulled her behind a nearby rock.

Three seconds later, a huge explosion rocked the clearing. The brilliant flash lit up a scene of utter chaos as those Indians nearest to the fire were blasted apart. Arms, legs and other unrecognizable bits flew in all directions. Jane buried her head in Will's shoulder. She screamed as a moccasined appendage struck her shoulder, splashing blood and gore over her beautiful but terrified features.

Will hugged her tight. It was a good feeling. But one he would have to forgo. He knew that seasoned warriors like these would soon regain control. And their desire for revenge would be swift and certain.

'Come on,' he urged, dragging the girl to her feet. They headed back down the trail. 'We ain't got much time.'

Thankfully there was now sufficient light to see by. He threw a quick glance over to the far side of the clearing. Ben Cassidy had recovered his pistol and was busy hauling off at the blood-streaked throng.

'Leave that,' shouted Will, gesticulating for his partner to join him. 'We need to put some distance between them an' us afore they recover.'

Ben raised a hand in acknowledement before launching a final salvo at the nearest rebel.

It was one shot too many. An arrow buried itself in his shoulder, spinning him round like a child's top. The Indians were quickly regrouping. Ben gasped, his face creased in pain. As he sank to the sandy floor, his right hand reached out for the deadly shaft.

Seeing his partner in dire straits, Will spoke quickly to the girl.

'Follow this trail down through the draw for two hundred yards. You'll find two horses tied to a yucca. Wait there for us.'

'What if . . ?' she began.

'Don't even think on it,' snapped Will, pushing her unceremoniously down the brush-strewn draw. 'Now get movin'. Them durned redskins'll be on us afore long.' Then he relented, offering her a brief yet poignant glimpse of the human being that existed beneath the tough exterior. 'If me and Ben don't make it. . .' he handed her a small up-and-over derringer. '. . . this here gun has two bullets.' There was no need to elaborate further. The icy mask returned.

Jane swallowed hard, then nodded. She understood.

Will swivelled on his heel. Before he could move, she gripped his arm.

'Good luck,' she murmured, her dark eyes filling up. Her petition met with a slight softening of the tight jaw, a thawing of the steely resolve. Then he was hurrying back along the trail, sixgun cocked and ready.

Gritting his teeth against the waves of nausea that threatened to engulf him, Ben Cassidy made one last effort to raise and fire the Colt double-action revolver. But the stiff trigger defeated him. His head slumped. This was the end. He was finished.

But not quite.

The injured man suddenly felt himself being lifted, his

142

punctured body thrown over the shoulder of his rescuer. The pain was intense as the arrow twisted in his bloodied shoulder.

'Sorry, pard,' apologized a breathless Will Brennan, 'but this ain't no time for the gentle approach.' Two rapid shots sent further pursuing Indians scuttling for cover. Then Will was hurrying back down the draw as fast as his heavy burden would allow. Thorny tendrils reached out, plucking at exposed flesh. Sharp-edged outcrops jarred his legs. Twice he stumbled, skinning his knuckles on protruding teeth of rock.

The two hundred yards back to where he had tethered the horses seemed like as many miles. Muscles straining, he ploughed on.

How much further?

Just when his aching legs were threatening to collapse, a scream immediately ahead made Will lurch to a halt. A blinding flash followed by a sharp report bounced off the surrounding rocks. His spinning head recognized it as emanating from the derringer. A tomahawk-wielding Navaho had been about to cleave his skull. Thanks to unerring accuracy, whether by luck or otherwise, the small but lethal shell had permanently removed the yelling pursuer from the chase.

But others were not far behind.

Expertly, Will eased the limp body from his stiff and aching back and laid Ben Cassidy on the ground.

'See to him, Jane, whilst I delay this lot for a spell.'

Tenderly, with tears dribbling down her dust-caked cheek, she dabbed at her fiancé's sweat-stained face with a damp necker. It was ashen, his lips turning blue. Not a good sign.

Meanwhile, Will grabbed the Winchester from its saddle boot. With ruthless efficiency he levered and triggered off a dozen shots in as many seconds. Flame and lead spat from the carbine, whining across the breadth of the canyon like angry hornets. None found its target. But the withering fusillade was enough to deter the renegades from venturing too close. They all dived for cover.

'That oughta keep their heads down,' snorted Will, squinting back up the trail. 'At least, long enough for us to eat some dust.'

He then helped Jane to lift the injured man into the saddle before mounting up behind.

'We'll have to ride double. You take the other cayuse.'

As soon as the girl was in the saddle, Will slapped the animal on its hindquarters with the flat of his hand. Snorting and neighing at the unexpected assault on its rump, the horse leapt forward with Jane clinging on precariously.

'Now ride as if the hounds of hell were snapping at your tail,' he yelled, spurring his own horse forward. The unaccustomed extra weight meant that he quickly fell behind Jane. With the injured Cassidy swaying like some drink-soused cowpoke on pay-day, it took all Will's efforts to prevent him from sliding out of the saddle. He knew that if they were going to survive, a stand would have to be made sooner or later.

A gleam crept into Will Brennan's narrowed gaze. He knew just the place.

Their progress quickly slowed amidst the chaotic disorder of scrub and loose boulders that littered the canyon floor. After four hours of being pushed to its limits, the overloaded dun mare was showing signs of total exhaustion. Nostrils flaring, blood seeping from its mouth, it stumbled ever more frequently.

'Only another mile, old gal,' Will whispered gently

coaxing the distraught beast onward. 'You can make it.' Bloodshot eyes flickered. A low muted sound more like a strained cough acknowledged the entreaty. Both horse and rider had established a trusting partnership over many years. It now looked certain that this was approaching its finale. Will's voice cracked with suppressed emotion as he continued muttering words of encouragement.

Just as their goal hove into sight, Will felt a gut-wrenching tremor ripple through the horse's lathered torso. Then it staggered to a halt, slumped forward on to its fetlocks and keeled over, throwing the two riders to one side.

Much as he felt the need to grieve for his old friend, there was no time for displays of sentiment. Stealing himself, Will lifted the Colt revolver from its holster and thumbed back the hammer. A moment of indecision, then the gun exploded in his hand. The reek of cordite mingled with excreta as the sphincter muscle collapsed.

But Will had other things on his mind.

Not daring to lay eyes on the horse still quivering in its death throes, he shaded his eyes against the glare of the sun and peered back up the trail. A cloud of red dust told him that the renegade Navahos were hot on their tail. Cast afoot with a badly wounded partner in tow, he estimated that it would only be a matter of twenty minutes or so before they caught up.

'Help me get this fella into the cave.' Will's blunt command was received with a mixture of perplexity and annoyance by Jane Fanshaw.

Who did this guy think he was, ordering her about? And where was the cave?

He responded to her sharp look of irritation by pointing to the base of the rock wall fifty feet above valley level where the bank of loose shale began.

Following his direction, eyes half-closed, she could just make out a dark opening. The small gap in the sandstone was almost hidden by a clump of mesquite and thorn. Her mouth fell open. Dark eyes bulged as recognition dawned.

Montezuma's cave!

TWELVE

UNEXPECTED BREAKTHROUGH

'How did you know about this?'

'I'll tell you later. Now help me with Ben.' Will's brusque retort was a sharp reminder of their precarious situation. Slipping and sliding up the shifting bank of scree, they eventually manhandled the barely conscious man into the shelter of the cave. Jane looked around. Nothing had changed. Why should it? The cave had lain undiscovered for over three centuries.

After they had made Ben Cassidy as comfortable as their position allowed, Will returned to the horses and removed the two rifles, water bottles and his saddle-bags, which contained spare food and ammunition.

He settled down behind a boulder near the entrance and reloaded his Winchester. Then he awaited the arrival of their pursuers.

He sensed a movement behind him.

'Do you think we will get out of this in one piece?' The husky shake in her voice was enough to inform Will that

Jane Fanshaw was scared. And with good reason. They were trapped. Them sons of bitches could wait out there indefinitely until they died of thirst. Cassidy would be first. Even now, he stood little chance without the attentions of a doctor. Then the girl would succumb.

And if they ran out of ammunition before then? He promised himself to save a final bullet for her.

But all this he kept to himself.

'Sure thing, ma'am.' His chirpy reply belied all that he was thinking. 'We can last out here for a good few days. Them savages'll git tired of hangin' around. 'Sides, they have other fish to fry.' He was referring to the Navajos' burning desire for revenge against their sworn enemies. 'Them Utes will be movin' on soon, which means Stalking Bear will want to attack their camp while he still has the chance.'

The truth was somewhat different. Following the rescue of the white woman, Stalking Bear would have lost face in the eyes of his men. Reinstatement of that authority was now of paramount importance. Failure and he would be scorned. His men would desert, or another brave would challenge his leadership. Either way it would be a death knell for the Navajo chief.

Jane leaned over and unscrewed the cap from one of the water bottles.

'One swallow only,' said Will quietly, holding her gaze. 'That's all the water we got.'

A groan from her wounded fiancé brought their dire position into stark perspective. But this was not the time to feel sorry for herself. With a monumental effort, she fought off the panic, the feeling of helplessness, that threatened to overwhelm her.

A silence settled over the tiny refuge. It was a grim silence heavy with foreboding and devoid of warmth.

Waiting for the imminent arrival of the Indians played havoc with their already overwrought nerves.

Then a strange thought occurred to Jane Fanshaw. Her pert nose wrinkled.

'How did you know about this cave?' she queried.

Will's sweat-stained features cracked in a loose smile.

'The map,' he said, removing the crumpled piece of paper from his shirt pocket. 'Duke Miller was carryin' it. Trapper Dan told me the full story of the Indian attack just before he died.'

Jane gasped on hearing this distressing news.

'Heggerty's dead?' she exclaimed.

'Them ants did fer him,' sighed Will, shaking his head. Maybe if they came out of this alive he would tell her about his relationship to the hunter. 'Along with the blistering heat he didn't stand a chance.'

'He saved my life, you know. Threw himself across my body when the Indians started that rock fall.' Her voice had sunk to a low sob as tears welled up. 'He could have saved his own skin. But he took the pounding in my place.'

Just then a whooping announced the arrival of the pursuers. They had found Will's dead horse.

Jane wiped a sleeve across her face. She squared her narrow shoulders. A cold gleam, hard and flinty, now replaced the mournful dirge of self-pity.

'Give me that Marlin.' Her tone was icy cool, suggesting a fervid determination to go out in a spirited blaze of glory, if that was the way it had to be. She took hold of the long rifle. This was her fiancé's weapon of choice. Now it was hers. And this was not the first time she had fired it. Previously it had only been at paper targets on the shooting-range. But that was about to change.

'Here they come!' Will's quavering call to action was instinctive, a battle cry fuelled by the rush of pure adrenalin. 'Pick your target and make every shot count.'

Together, side by side, they faced the initial flurry. It was a ploy previously utilized on numerous occasions by Stalking Bear to gauge the strength of his opponents. Sometimes, men were lost. But that was a risk he was prepared to take. This time he knew his enemy numbered only three, and one of those was badly wounded. And holed up in the cave, there was no way out.

The Navajo chieftain needed to assert his authority by means of a quick and decisive attack. The first rush would waste valuable ammunition of his opponents. Well versed in the art of skirmishing, the Indians made full use of the cluttered array of boulders and stunted juniper trees. Like ghosts they flitted from rock to rock barely showing themselves but drawing a fusillade of answering fire from the defenders. The seemed but hazy phantoms dancing on the hot breeze, and vanished just as quickly.

Will snapped off a couple of shots to his left when a scraping of shale drew his attention. Splinters chipped off the boulder but there was no answering scream of pain to indicate he had scored a hit.

Blasting away with the Marlin, Jane was luckier. One redskin, attempting to sneak up the edge of the scree slope found himself caught in the open, and staring down the barrel of the rifle. Malevolent eyes fixed on to the girl in a mesmeric embrace. For the briefest of instants Jane hesitated.

'Pull the trigger!'

The urgent bark in her ear, forceful and compelling, broke the spell. The rosewood stock bucked against her shoulder as the lethal bullet flew inexorably to its target. A loose smile slid across Jane's satin features. All that training on the range had finally paid dividends.

But already the attackers were pulling back to regroup.

Although fear was squeezing her insides, Jane was strangely exhilarated following her first taste of blood. Her hands were shaking, teeth chattering. Then she uttered a harsh yarraping cheer.

'I got one, didn't I? I shot him plumb centre.' A crazed inane sort of grin followed the excited pronouncement. Her eyes, glassy and staring, blazed with a fierce intensity.

Will knew the signs. Roughly and without preamble, he grabbed the girl's slim shoulders and attempted to shake some sense into her.

'Pull yourself together, girl,' he snapped. 'This ain't no Sunday turkey-shoot. Them savages will skin us alive if we're taken. And that ain't no idle speculation. It's the goldarned truth.'

Slowly Jane's fevered expression waned, then subsided as the reality of their desperate predicament became all too clear.

'I'm sorry,' she apologized, slumping against the cold wall of the cave. 'I just got carried away for the moment.'

Will's stiff expression softened, the hard edged tone became quieter but no less urgent.

'I can understand how you feel,' he said. 'Just so's you understand that . . .' Knowing what his next words would mean, Will's outpouring faltered.

'Yes?'

'Well . . . that our chances of getting out of this mess are pretty slim.'

'But you said . . .'

'I know what I said. Truth is we're in one helluva fix.'

He then peered down at the recumbent figure of Ben Cassidy. The wounded man's skin had taken on a waxy grey pallor. 'And Ben has even less of a chance than us.'

'Is he . . . you know?' Her hoarse whisper faltered.

'Not yet. But without professional help, he's a goner for

sure. That wound is festering.' He lifted his wide-brimmed hat, wiped the sweat from his brow, and gave the girl a keen look.

But before he could say any more, a concentrated barrage of rifle and pistol fire erupted from below. Bullets zipped and whined around the narrow confines of the cave entrance, seeking them out. They dived to the floor and hugged the hard ground.

For ten minutes the Indians continued to pepper the cave with lead. Chips of broken rock cuffed and pummelled their cowering bodies.

'Is there no way out of here?' Will hollered in desperation above the screeching din. Eyes screwed up, he tried ineffectually to penetrate the dark passage stretching away into the bowels of the mountain. 'How far back does it stretch?'

'About fifty yards,' replied Jane. 'But it's blocked off. My father and I had only just checked it out when you saved us from that mountain lion.'

Will heaved a weary sigh.

'That'll have to be my new nickname.'

'What?'

'Brennan the Hero – champion of damsels in distress.'

Jane couldn't help but laugh. For a brief second her face lit up, the innate beauty shining through.

As abruptly as it had commenced, the firing ceased. The silence was almost tangible after the deafening assault on the ears.

Then, from without, a deep baritone split the ether. Slow and ponderous, the exaggerated phrasing was all the more chilling.

'Can you hear me, white eyes?'

'I hear you!' responded Will.

'What do they call you?'

152

'The name's *Lucky* Will Brennan,' returned Will, placing a vigorous emphasis on his nickname.

The Indian emitted a gravelly cackle that bounced off the canyon walls. Hollow and sinister, it resonated absolute menace, forcing the hairs on Will's neck to stand on end.

'Then it would seem your luck has run out, Mr Brennan. You cannot escape me now. And soon it will be night. You and the girl will be at my mercy. Think well on this, Lucky Will Brennan. And be sure that none of you will see another daybreak.'

The Indians then settled down to await the onset of night.

'How much ammunition have you?' asked Jane extending an open palm to reveal her own paltry supply – five brass cartridges winked at her in the afternoon sun.

Will open his saddle-bag and felt inside. A grim cast stole across the weathered countenance.

'That does it, then,' he snorted, 'We ain't got a snowball's chance in hell if they rush us again.' Face set in concrete, his mind was racing. What to do now?

Then he made a decision. 'I aim to take a peek at the end of this tunnel and see for myself if there's a way out.' He handed his Winchester to the girl. The Marlin might well have greater accuracy over distance but it lacked the rapid-fire advantage of the lever-action carbines. 'You stay here and keep watch.'

'But I told you, it's blocked up,' insisted the girl.

'Have you any other suggestions?'

A blank look accompanied the curt head-shake.

He wiped a vesta on his pants and scrambled along the narrow passage aided by the dim light. At the end he came upon the same blockage encountered by Jane and her late father. Lighting up the discarded torch left by Blake

Fanshaw, he was able to inspect the end of the chamber in more detail – and with more than a hint of desperation in his fumblings.

Scrambling about on hands and knees at the base of the apparently solid rock wall, Will felt a slight waft of cool air on his hand. His back stiffened. He grabbed at the firebrand and held it close to the source of the faint zephyr, then held his breath.

At first nothing, then a hesitant flicker. Only slight but enough to prove that the passage continued beyond this immediate obstacle. Encouraged by this momentous discovery, Will clawed at the boulders piled up to the rough ceiling little more than a foot above his head. They were heavy and cumbersome, but the conviction of what failure would soon deliver lent a fervid spur to his endeavours.

They say that desperation turns a frail man into a raging Colossus. Will Brennan was certainly no weakling but during the next half-hour, he discovered muscles he never knew existed. Sweat poured down his face, dust choked his throat. But there was no let-up. The pile of stones and rubble hefted into the main body of the cave grew slowly but surely.

'What's going on down there?'

Jane's anxious query echoed down the narrow tunnel.

'Give me ten minutes and I'll be able to tell you,' responded Will. Another half-hour passed. Just as Will was beginning to think he was fighting a losing battle, he stumbled forward, his outstretched hand clawing at a hole no bigger than his fist.

But it was enough. He was through. Elation, excitement, relief – a whole amalgam of euphoric feelings engulfed him simultaneously. Any attempt to cast an eye into the black void was instantly curtailed by a putrid stench emanating from the tiny fissure. He drew back coughing and spluttering.

'What in hell's teeth is that!' he exclaimed, clutching a hand to his nose, hoping in some way to alleviate the gagging odour. Quickly he shuffled back to the cave entrance to relate the vital news to Jane.

'Does this mean we can escape?' A trace of disbelief caught in her throat.

'Looks like it. I've only made a small hole so far, but the signs are good.' Then a dark frown crossed his dirt-streaked features. 'There's one god-awful stench comin' from the other side.'

Together, they returned to the barrier. Jane helped with the Herculean task of enlarging the hole as much as she was able. It was a further hour before a sufficiently large aperture was excavated enabling Will to squeeze through.

'I was right,' he shouted back excitedly. 'The tunnel continues on this side. Pass me the torch.'

A startled gasp intermingled with a touch of the macabre punched through the enlarged hole.

'What's wrong, Will?' Jane blurted out her concern. 'What have you found?'

'Don't worry!' came back the shaky response. 'Everything's all right. It's just that . . .' He hesitated.

'Yes?'

'. . . I've found where that stink was coming from.'

Only the husky rasp of heavy breathing filtered from the opening.

'Well, don't keep it to yourself.' Jane's impatient reaction prompted him to continue.

'Two skeletons . . . clinging together . . . just like lovers.'

Without further prompting, Jane wriggled through the hole to join him.

Side by side, they both stared agape at the bizarre revelation. Jane had at last uncovered the secret of Montezuma's epic journey. So where was the treasure that was supposedly interred here? She grabbed the torch from Will and wafted it around the small hidden chamber.

'What d'you make of it?' asked Will, curiosity asserting itself above the urgent need to escape.

Jane drew herself up, the consummate archaeologist surging to the fore.

'I can only assume that the treasure was discovered by grave robbers some time after it was first secreted here. Perhaps they were able to reach it from that direction.' She nodded towards the black tunnel. 'It would certainly make sense.'

Then her gaze shifted back to the skeletons. Shreds of cloth still clung to the dry bones. It was as if they had gone to sleep and never awakened. A sense of awe imbued her next supposition. 'This could very well be the son of the great Montezuma. The one who made that momentous journey all the way from Mexico to safeguard the heritage of Aztlan. It was common practice in those days for important dignitaries to be buried with their loved ones. Such an arduous trek must have been too much for him.'

Ever the pragmatist, Will's instinct for their survival took over.

'There is no way that we're gonna end up the same way.' His tone was firm and decisive. 'We'll go back and fix Ben up. Between the two of us, we oughta be able to pull him through the hole. Then we'll turn the tables on Stalking Bear.'

On their return to the cave entrance, it was patently obvious to Will that his partner was a goner. Blood dribbled from the open mouth. Dead eyes stared back vacantly.

'I'm sorry, Jane,' he mouthed quietly. 'I know he loved you a great deal.'

Jane burst into tears, burying her face in Will's shoulder. A shiver rippled down his spine. He stroked her lustrous hair, relishing the close contact.

Maybe. Just maybe if they could get out of this mess.

A movement across the canyon caught his attention. Them pesky redskins looked as if they were on the move again. Gently, almost reluctantly, he prised himself out of the girl's embrace. He removed his coat and placed it reverently over the dead man.

'Time we made ourselves scarce,' he said, levering a cartridge into the breech of the Winchester. Triggering three shots in rapid succession, he had the satisfaction of striking lucky. A moment of careless exposure proved fatal for one renegade. 'That should give 'em somethin' to think on. They won't be so quick to rush us now.'

With a last bleary-eyed glance towards her fiancé Jane followed Will back down the tunnel. They squirmed through the low aperture, then proceeded along the level passage beyond. It was more constricted than the outer passage and they were forced to bend low to avoid painful contact with the roof.

Even under such hazardous conditions, Jane's professional interest remained.

'We must be the first humans to enter this burial chamber in centuries. A pity about the treasure, though. But at least I've finally solved the legend. My father can rest in peace now.'

Slowly they began their own trek to locate the exit. It might well be blocked, impossible to circumvent. Will shivered. That scenario didn't bear thinking about. Water seeping from above trickled down the rough-hewn walls dripping from the roof. It made the uneven floor slippery.

After two hours of struggling along the constricted passage, Jane's left ankle twisted on a greasy rock. She cried out in pain, slumping to the ground. The wetness soaking into her clothes was ignored.

They rested for ten minutes, then carried on with Will supporting her. But progress was much slower now. Time passed in a hazy recollection of stabbing torment for Jane. At last she could go no further. Will lit one of his few remaining vestas and peered down at his watch. He was surprised it was still going.

The time read 11.15.

It was well past sundown. In this subterranean gallery of perpetual darkness, day and night meant nothing. Those redskins would have stormed the cave by now. Will, however, was confident they would not have continued the pursuit along the underground passage. Indians hated confined spaces.

Both utterly exhausted, the two fugitives settled down with backs against the rough wall. Thankfully, due to their exhausted state, sleep came easy.

Next morning, they carried on. The tallow brand had long since burnt itself out. They were now purely reliant on touch. It was only Will's constant encouragement that kept Jane going. Panic threatened to overwhelm her at ever more frequent intervals.

When they had almost given up hope of survival, the thick black treacle slowly melted to a dull grey. Then suddenly, on rounding the next bend, they stumbled out into brilliant sunlight. The contrast with their Stygian tomb was absolute.

Clinging to each other, both gave thanks to God. They kissed, laughed, swallowed up by ecstatic feelings of rapture, wallowing in the pure joy of their release. Sinking back down to earth, they gazed around trying to assess where in fact they had ended up.

The cave's back entrance was located one hundred feet above the floor of a broad canyon. It seemed somehow familiar. Then Will noticed a few horses munching on clumps of dry gramma grass.

His eyes widened. This had to be the Indian encampment. Wisps of smoke drifted from the embers of the fire. And horses. They must be those left by the Indians killed during the rescue.

Carefully, Will helped Jane down the rough shale slope to valley level. They secured a pair of horses, mounted up and spurred towards the head of the canyon in the opposite direction from which they had first arrived. Overhead, the sun wore a broad grin. The light breeze chuckled at their good fortune.

'Maybe, after all that's happened, *I* should call you Lucky Brennan as well,' suggested Jane.

The tall man offered a wry smile.

'You better believe it, ma'am,' he replied, casually handing her a small leather pouch. 'Take a look inside.'

Jane eyed him askance, then opened the ancient bag and removed the contents. Her dark eyes opened wide. Staring back at her was a solid gold pendant.

All that remained of Montezuma's legacy.

'At least you're now sure it really did exist,' said Will, reaching out to take her hand. Their eyes met.

Was that more than just a hint of gratitude he could see? Only time would tell.